To Norman (

TERRORISTS BEGUILED

BY

PETER HOGG

With best wishes
from
Mary & Peter

TERRORISTS BEGUILED

PETER HOGG

~~~ BrightSparkPublishing ~.co.uk

DEDICATED
TO
MY WIFE
MARY

Designed, typeset, printed, and bound completely in-house
By BrightSpark Publishing,
Unit 11
The Wards
New Elgin
ELGIN
IV30 6AA

Telephone 01343 544336
Or mobile 07967 178224

CHAPTER ONE

To say the least, Stan Watson was depressed. His whole life, he felt, was far from complete. He was sitting in a pub drinking a pint of his favourite beer, which, although great to consume, was something he was somehow not getting any enjoyment out of. The lack of company had perhaps something to do with it, as, for some reason, none of his pals had joined him. But it was really quite silly, of course, to wonder *why* they had not appeared: they were all working, Stan was not! He and his wife had worked together for many years, happily; but then, as often happens, the Fates had conspired against them, for tragedy struck when she became involved in a disastrous road accident, resulting in her far too early death.

At this time of the morning, Stan always read his favourite newspaper. Before turning to the football page, Stan glanced cursorily at the latest proposals for terrorism laws. Although the loss of lives in the recent atrocities was confined to London, the whole of the United Kingdom was shocked to the core by the number of deaths in the capital city. Actions such as this had not occurred since the second World

War, when London in particular had been so badly hit by bombs and later by rockets and other missiles. At least at that time there had always been the opportunity for the Brits to retaliate by bombing the countries from which the carriers of these weapons came. Now, innocent people were being killed by unknown suicidal murderers. The right sort of litigation was needed and that had to be of a type ensuring that the training of the killers and their planners were detected prior to any nefarious action taking place. At this stage of his life, Stan was not really deeply interested in the prompt introduction of fresh legislation, but all the outside pages of the newspapers were reporting on the controversial 'Prevention of Terrorism Bill' which, despite its power restrictions, was, at least showing that the House of Lords could, after all, seriously challenge the House of Commons.

As he was reading of the cowardly murders, a memory of an event that had occurred overseas many years ago came to mind. Stan and three R.A.F. Pals had been sitting on the beach of a near equatorial country after having been for a swim to get away from the quite unbearable and most powerful sunshine they had ever known. Suddenly, they were joined by an Army Officer of a reasonable rank - he had forgotten what, but he remembered it outranked him. They had previously seen him exploring the sea shore.

"Come on boys! Further along the beach there is a wooden boat of heavy timber, anchored in the sea by its weight. Help me getting it float further out."

All the R.A.F. boys had seen it stationary before, perhaps two miles away. Without a suitable rank, they were unable to refuse but they all knew that his request was unachievable. They reached it finally but the surf was too powerful for five people to push it into deeper water. If it were moved there was also the risk of the heavy timber being forced, by the strength of the sea, into onè of its pushers intent on its floating. Then, as though this little event was occurring as an exciting film scene, there appeared something like forty to fifty Africans charging over the sand hills. Some looked as though they were armed with perhaps a few truncheons or spears.

On seeing this, the army leader cried out. "Run boys, run for your lives!" He charged away followed by three of the R.A.F. lads.

Stan, the fourth lad, realised that they could easily be caught by some of those brought up in a climate of intense heat, refused to run. No way was he going to flee! He was quickly surrounded by a ring of the African villagers. But to Stan's intense surprise, they all sat down, saying nothing. In a daze of amazement, Stan followed suit. Still nothing was said. But then one of them walked to Stan, proffered a cigarette and insisted that the white man smoked it. Unfortunately, Stan did not have any of his own cigarettes to reciprocate but this did not seem to matter - it was surely their eqivalent of the native Americans' 'Peace Pipe'.

For well over an hour, Stan had to accept cigarettes from those who wanted to display their hospitality. Then it was time for him to part company from them, so he thanked all the Africans for their hospitality by shaking hands with all of them, helping, he hoped, to establish a friendship for the future.

He then returned back along the beach and was pleased to

be able to join his three friends, who were amazed to see him still alive and grateful that he had engendered a rapport with the natives.

His thoughts on some of his past life were a great help to his present life. Stan's mind soon centred on Madge, his late wife. If only she were sitting next to him enjoying her favourite drink, a glass of sherry. There was nobody else in the bar, so he raised his pint of bitter and, in his normal speaking voice said, "Oh! I do love you my darling wife. May God be with you."

It was now almost as though they were, in reality sitting together, because a voice seemed to come back, "I love you too Stan and always will. May you have peace and enjoy your life.'

Forcing himself to banish this ghostly voice, thoughts came back to Stan to talk about the vital issues in his life nowadays - which involved the progress of his favourite game of football. Whether or not certain players should be in his first team was always a damned good topic, but, of course, not having his friends as mentioned before was not helpful. Still uppermost in his mind was the fact that, just a few days ago someone on the opposite side of the road had quickly crossed over and taken a photograph of him entering the pub. He had never seen the guy before and he objected, most strongly, to strangers pointing cameras at him. If only Madge were there she was always able to make something out of strange occurrences, to make the inexplicable seem commonplace. Never mind. He mused that once upon a time football scouts tried to find prospective players for his team - if only! A pity those days were over. He laughed at his own daydream. Another pint might help! It usually did!

Suddenly, a youngish, strongly built, foreign looking chap entered the pub and walked quickly to his table. "Mind if I join you, mate." he said.

"No" said Stan, thinking, *But only if you can talk football, but, in any case, what the hell do you want?*

"What is it, bitter or lager?"

"Bitter will do fine."

After the first slug of ice cold fluid made its way down south, the man said:

"How would you like to make some money?"

Stan looked at him suspiciously. "Oh, yeah? Doing what?"

"It's quite simple. You can have an all paid return holiday trip to the Baltic Sea, plus a payment of £5,000."

"Ah! Get lost! You must think that I'm a bloody nut!"

"On the contrary. All you have to do is to occupy an inside cabin and have all your meals delivered therein. The ship belongs to the Nordic Lines. It will stop at Tallinn. You will then go ashore. A stranger will mention a password, previously notified to you. You will then tell him your cabin number and hand over your boarding pass. This will be followed by the presentation of a train ticket for Calais, followed by a ticket for Dover. You will use them. On leaving the cross channel ship, proceed to and enter the men's conveniences, situated on the road leading from the dock area. Inside, you will find a man, standing near the wash bowls. He will be dressed in a blue shirt and denims. He will give you £5,000 and tell you that you may travel to your home."

Alter a short interval of silence, during which Stan realised that it would ease a bit of the boredom, Stan smiled and with a glint of expectation in his eyes said, "I'll do it - but for £10,000 and nothing less."

"My good friend, you are on dangerous grounds. You have been selected specially for this job. You have a past unknown to the police, but known to us. It is an event which occurred several years ago. I will not go into details but, as I am sure you are perfectly aware, a smuggling offence carries a sentence of imprisonment! Now, having been given certain information by us, you could find yourself in a dangerous situation. I am prepared to make arrangements for you to be paid £7,000. If you refuse to accept that amount, the predicament which I mentioned will come into force."

"Are you blackmailing me?"

"Correct - not wrong!"

"You scum!"

"Perhaps in your eyes, but not in others! But you have no option."

Stan realised that the man was right - he didn't have any option. "You win."

"Good. Specific instructions will be given later."

The ship sailed into harbour and Stan was the first to walk across the jetty. It was a fine, sunny morning and he proceeded onwards to the nearby road. A figure stood there waiting for him. As Stan drew nearer, he became astounded to see that, not only was he dressed similarly to the stranger, but their facial appearances and heights pretty well matched each other. He must have an infamous past to adopt an unusual procedure such as this. Discounting any modesty, perhaps his looks were worth simulating!

The stranger said immediately. "Our password, of which you have already been notified is 'Ocean'. Now hand over your boarding pass and tell me your cabin number You will travel to Russia and Germany before getting a train. You will go at once to the places indicated. A cash allowance is included to meet any travel expenses."

"My cabin number is 310. When am I going to get paid?"

"As instructed you will be paid immediately you reach Dover."

The stranger turned away and walked into the city. He would board the ship when many of the passengers were returning to the ship.

Stan made for the nearest travel shop for information about the railway station. Armed with his travel tickets and information on the best journey to take, he found that the route available was most enjoyable. The scenery, in particular, was a joy to behold. He realised then that it was time that he began to sort out his life. His investments rewarded him with an income sufficient enough, at his age to learn, where possible, that many parts of the world were waiting to be visited.

It did not take him long to arrive at Calais and the journey across the Channel was calm and of interest As expected, his passport enabled him to arrive in Dover without any difficulty. He left the ship with other passengers and, on leaving the dock area, it did not take him long to spot the nearest gents' conveniences, a single person cubicle. He headed towards it

"Ah hell!" he muttered, then, thinking to himself: *Everything has gone well but why does that guy, walking in front, have to visit the toilet now? I'll have to wait before I can get my hands on the £7,000. I'd better stand out of sight, in this doorway, until he comes out.*

After a few seconds, a man dashed out of the conveniences and ran to a car parked further along the road. Quickly, he opened its door and sped away.

"I'm sure that's not the chap that went inside." mused Stan. With a feeling of a slight apprehension he hesitated at the door and, finally, pushed it open.

"Oh my God!" he said. A man lay sprawled across the floor bleeding profusely from a chest wound. He knelt down but it was too late to stop the bleeding or give any other help. The inside of his pockets had been pulled out. They were now soaked in blood and, presumably, they had been searched in order to find any money or documents. There was no sign of a knife or any other weapon.

"Oh hell! That man must have thought this poor bugger was me! I must get away quickly." He dashed back to the dock area to retrieve his car still parked in the ship's public enclosure.

Getting home took longer than he had envisaged. It was actually normal for getting to the other side of London but he was weighed down by <u>thinking</u> of the poor guy lying dead on the lavatory floor. What should he do when he arrived home? How could he explain to the police that he had been asked to visit the toilets for the purpose of collecting £7,000. More important, though, was taking into account the fact that the man immediately preceding him had been horribly slaughtered. What if the sharp dagger had been thrust into *his* body? He felt sick with horror. He knew he had been intended to be the recipient of the vicious blow.

It was highly likely that the organiser of the Baltic trip knew his home address. He must get away quickly. Gathering all his necessary clothing and making financial arrangements had become vital but there were other things to be done, such as, the destruction of written addresses and the removal of the telephone numbers of friends and relatives. Despite these drawbacks, he was still able to escape from his home within an hour or so.

Soon, the ship from the holiday trip to the Baltic arrived back in Dover. The passengers were released in batches according to the numbers of their cabins. Their luggage was waiting on the quay together with buses for London and other major areas. A man, very much the image of Stan, asked one of the ship's attendants for his case to be taken to the London bus. With a broad smile on his face he took a seat at the rear of the bus. Prior to leaving the ship, he had obviously thought about disposing of the ship's papers and within a couple of seconds he had given the ship's pass to one of the purser's officials. As had been expected, no one on the quay had been asked to see his passport His true identity was unknown.

CHAPTER TWO

Stan was on the M4 heading west.

He wished that Madge had been with him. She was always full of good humour. Her laughter was so infectious too. If only the approaching driver had not driven to her side of the road with great speed and hit her full on. Her car was a complete wreck and she had died right away. At least the court had given the drunken driver a long prison sentence but what was the use of that? Now, there was no Madge to make him see the funny side of life. She had been brought up in North Wales. A country that she loved so much. To him, the language was so cute but, try as she could, she was unable to make him understand it. Each morning she would wake him up first, kiss and tickle him and whisper 'bore da' in his ear. If only she was in the car, sitting alongside. By now she would have outlined a plan to make him safe from being detected by the guy in the pub.

How the hell did anyone know about the time that he had driven a load of cocaine from a cove near to Fishguard. This must have been the origin of the threat, by that damned guy in the pub, to give information to the police. At the time, Stan knew little about the offence. He had foolishly agreed to deliver it to some address in Birmingham. Madge, with her knowledge of Wales, had loaded him with details about some of the quiet roads from Fishguard to the address. But this was many years ago. Thanks to her, the journey was uneventful and delivery was made without recognition of anyone of importance and yet someone had taken note of his appearance. Dear Madge had arranged that, immediately, on receiving confirmation of his delivery she would surreptitiously telephone the Birmingham police of the drug load. A successful seizure was made but luckily the address of the deliverer was never discovered.

There and then he promised his wife never to attempt the smuggling of drugs or goods again.

Now he had to think very carefully about a suitable place to live and perhaps to change his name. The town of Reading was just ahead and a day or two's stay at a hotel would give him a period of relaxation and time to give serious thought to his future life. He turned off the road and approached Reading. He sighted a most delightful looking hotel surrounded by trees and well kept gardens. It looked restful and turned out to be reasonably priced. He signed in for two days under the name of 'John Heed' On reflection later on he was completely mystified as to why he invented that name!

He was pleased with the comfort of the room and, after an enjoyable dinner he retired early to bed. He fell asleep immediately but awoke soon after midnight. Troublesome thoughts came to his mind that someone had entered the country without any immigration documentation. The Tallinn man was copying his looks and, to make matters worse, was, ostensibly, wearing his clothes. It was obvious that a form of disguise had been, for him, important. What had he done in the past to justify an entry to this country with the least possible awareness by the Immigration authorities and, possibly, the police? Why? Was he a criminal? A terrorists? Perhaps even the leader of a terrorist organisation?

Madge came back to his thoughts. At the very least, he had been extremely lucky. A large farm, in North Wales, had been owned by her father. After his death and, that of her mother, it had been bequeathed to Madge. She sold it and received a large sum of money. He, in his turn, had become the benefactor of that wealth. Judging by its current value, the money had been well invested. Stan was by nature, a very careful spender. His last thoughts, before returning hack to sleep, were that perhaps a nice girl was waiting somewhere to become his wife. Life went on - which Madge would understand.

On entering the breakfast room, the following morning, he was welcomed by a fellow guest who was reading one of that morning's newspapers. He raised his head and wished Stan a good morning. "That was a terrible murder at Dover, wasn't it?"

"Oh!" said Stan, "I've not read about it yet."

"A man went into a Gents and was brutally murdered. The police have asked for help from anyone in the vicinity. A woman has come forward to say that she saw a man leaving the building and then racing to get into his car further up the road. He sped up the road far too quickly and was breaking the speed limit. Strangely, within a minute or two, another man followed suit and ran to get his, which had been left in the port's public car space. He also disappeared at full speed, but went in a different direction."

'That's awful. I hope that they can catch the killer pretty quickly. It's frightening to hear that this can happen to our once peaceful country."

"And sad too. He was father to two children as well. Yes, as you say, what an age we live in," he groaned as he left the room.

Stan hurried through his breakfast and decided to look around the town. Strolling around and reading a newspaper, on a relatively quiet morning, encouraged Stan to think deeply about events so far. What about his home? He had been easily recognised when sitting in his favourite pub. Tallinn was the same too. The man who was impersonating him had had no difficulty. The only solution was to alter his looks. First, though, he must have a look around his house to see if anyone had been rummaging, with the hope of discovering a clue as to his whereabouts. It could well be, that in his desperation to avoid leaving anything that might lead to finding him, he had foolishly neglected a thorough check. But he was in a desperate hurry, or so he thought. He could not escape from the feeling that, if the previous day, he had been a target for killing, he still remained one.

He must get home and seek out his belongings. On no account must he leave anything that could divulge his whereabouts. Perhaps it would not take long for a night visit but what about his car? A woman in this morning's newspapers had already indicated that she had witnessed two men. separately dashing from the Dover toilets to make quick escapes in their cars. Had she studied and recorded his registration number and, already, given it to the police?

To deal with this situation he crossed the road to inspect a dealer's display of old and new cars. He told the dealer that he had sold his previous ear several months ago and now he could not remember its registration number. Also, he had lost his insurance certificate. After much bargaining, he bought his car of choice and obtained the appropriate insurance. (From any bargaining point of view he doubted if he had made an exemplary purchase!)

Although there was just sufficient lighting in the vicinity of his home, it was quite dark when he parked his car several roads away from his address. His front door was firmly closed but, quite by accident, a neighbour was closing his gate.

"Hello! Haven't seen you for a couple of days. Have you been on holiday?"

"No, not really. I've just had a few days away on business. I'm here to see if there's any important mail. I'm leaving again in a few minutes!"

"I'm always available on the phone. Let me know if I can be of any help."

"I shall! Many thanks."

To Stan's great relief, the house contents appeared undisturbed but, even so, he made a very careful examination of all the rooms and cupboards. After collecting a case and several items of clothing he left feeling more relaxed.

He made his way back to the car. Back at the hotel, he would give more thought to further planning.

CHAPTER THREE

Jim and Alan, occupying the Police car, were making their way out of Dover. They were discussing the achievements of their favourite football teams.

"What the hell!" shrieked Jim "That car's easily doing seventy miles and we are not yet out of the town. Catch the blighter!"

Alan put his foot down. They were soon out of the town but, even then, they topped ninety to keep pace. Finally, on a turn in the road, they managed to overtake and cause the driver to stop.

"Let me see your driving licence please sir." said Jim. "You were driving faster than the legal limit, both in and out of the town. What is your name?"

"I thought that I was driving at the normal speed. I haven't got my licence with me. I'm dashing to see my mother who is badly ill in hospital!"

"Would you please get out of the car and give me your name and driving licence. At once! I'm serious. Are you British?"

The man remained seated in his car. Jim shouted, "Alan can you give me a hand with this guy, please."

Alan came over, issued a caution and arrested him.

Meanwhile, Jim made a call to Dover headquarters. They drove back into the town commenting, with an air of curiosity, on the fact that there were two H.Q- cars sitting outside the public conveniences.

After the desk sergeant went through the normal procedures, he made arrangements for the man to occupy a prison cell and, later, to be taken to an interview room.

"Mr. Sharif, you are now in an interview room. Everything that is said in this room will be recorded. I am turning on the recorder now. I have to warn you that you are not obliged to say anything but anything yo do say will be taken down and may be given in evidence against you in a court of law, do you understand?" Sharif didn't answer. "Do you understand?" he repeated, to which Sharif nodded.

"Okay. You have been introduced to Mr. Hughes sitting next to you. He will act as your legal representative and if you are in doubt about anything said, he is there to advise you. I am Inspector Lewis and the policeman on my right is Inspector Barnes. Today's date is the 5th August 2005 and the time is ten thirty in the morning."

"You were arrested yesterday morning for exceeding, in your car, the speeding limit laid down by law, in Dover and on the roads outside the town. For that alleged offence and others, concerning a person found to be dead in one of Dover's public conveniences, you will be required to appear before a Court of Law. Now, will you please tell me where you live?"

"I don't have an address. I move around staying in lodges."

"Where did you lodge last night?"

"At a house in London. I have forgotten the name of the road."

"I low long have you been living there?"

"A couple of nights."

"And before that?"

"I can't remember the lodgings."

"Where do you come from?"

"The Middle East."

"But which country?"

"I've moved around a lot. Saudi and Pakistan."

"You've already produced your immigration papers. What's your work here?"

"I deliver food to shops."

"What shops?"

"Different shops."

"Mr Sharif, I'm not getting positive replies from you. It is imperative that I receive some information about your life in Britain. I have asked you about the shops to which you deliver food. Is the food which you normally deliver, of a type that you would obtain from a shop in Pakistan? Also would you tell me who owns the shops from which you obtain goods for delivery to other shops?"

"People from Pakistan."

"Are the deliveries sometimes made directly to people living in private houses?"

"No, never."

"On arrest you were carrying a loaded gun? You knew that was against the law?"

"No. I've had it here for a while. I was told that I

needed it to save myself from being killed by the people here."

"Who were these people whom you were told carried guns to kill you?"

"People I met in the streets."

"Do you realise that it is against the laws of this country to carry guns and that you can be imprisoned for carrying guns."

"No, I thought everyone carried guns."

"Your jacket was found to have traces of explosive material. Where was the explosive material from?"

"I don't know."

"You don't know?"

"It must be from people in the Metro."

"Metro? You have come from France? Did you live there?"

"Yes for a year or two."

"What did you do there?"

"I worked on a farm."

"Were you with friends?"

"Yes."

"Did you make explosives when you were there?"

"NO!"

"But there were traces of explosive material on your jacket. You have already said that it came from France. Did you and your friends make it?"

"No, we did not make it."

"Whilst staying in France, were you practising killing people?"

"I didn't need to practice." That was an arrogan slip

that the policeman leaped on.

"Do you carry a knife for that purpose?"

"No. I carry a knife to protect myself."

"What have you done with your knife?"

"I threw it away."

"When did you throw it away?"

"A while ago."

"When you were driving away from Dover had you been to the public toilets?"

A pause. "No."

"But a man matching your description was seen coming out of the toilets before you drove away."

"That wasn't me."

"Your jacket was marked with blood. We can prove that it was not your blood."

"Yes, it wasn't mine."

"Whose blood was it then?"

"I don't know."

"I think you do! I also believe that you went into the toilets and killed a man who was already there. For the purpose I think you used your own knife."

There was no reply to this statement.

"Mr Sharif, I believe that you are not telling me the truth. I put it to you that it was you who exited that toilet. Very shortly afterwards a man was found lying dead on the floor. His chest was covered in blood. I think that you were in the toilets and that you used your own knife to kill that man. Your fingerprints will place you there! Admit it, man!"

"OK I did go into the toilets. A man was lying on the floor bleeding badly. I ran to him and knelt down to see if I could help but it was too late. He was dead. Another man had rushed away from the toilets shortly before my arrival. It is he whom you must arrest and bring to court."

"Mr Sharif, do you realise that you are facing the possibility of a long term of imprisonment, if you are found guilty of murder? If you tell me truthfully who your associates are and what you are trying to achieve in Britain, I will do my best to make it known that, in our session of today, you have been helpful."

Sharif merely grunted his unwillingness to co-operate.

Having had enough, the policeman said: "It is now twelve fifteen and the end of the questioning for today. You will be escorted back to your cell."

CHAPTER FOUR

Stan's cousin lived in Kelso, north of the Scottish Border. It is a most delightful part of Scotland, with picturesque burns and rivers, tremendous views of green hills and, further east, a delightful coastline.

David's wife was a General Practitioner. They had two children. He worked for the Government but he was a little bit more than your ordinary, run of the mill Civil Servant. He had never spoken very much about his job but to Stan it was a very special one, or, more likely, perhaps a member of more than one Special branch or even M.I.5. or M.I.6. Jokingly, Stan would accuse him of working for the CIA but this would only cause him to roar with laughter. Certainly he often visited the United States. His father had been younger than that of Stan's but, in their youth, the cousins had been very close friends.

After a lot of thought. Stan decided to see if he could stay at his cousin's house and, if it were possible, see if he could obtain some advice on his current predicament. David had always been the person to solve any difficulties facing them when they were children. He would, of course have to relate all the problems of the previous days. His wife. Anne, was a great friend and ally. She went out of her way to make visitors feel at home.

To his surprise. David answered his telephone call. "Hi! Stranger. Haven't seen you for years. What about coming to 'Bonnie Scotland' for a great holiday. Not to be missed in a million years. Perhaps you'll give me a chance to beat you at golf."

"Hi! It's great to speak to you. How's Anne? Keeping well I hope - and the children of course?"

"Oh! They're all keeping fine. Far better for seeing you!"

"Would it be all right for me to come for a stay in a couple of days time?"

"Of course! We are all looking forward to seeing you. Cheers for now!"

Stan packed his belongings in the boot of his ear. In doing so, it dawned on him that he must not arrive with too many clothes thrown into the back of the car. He decided to cut across to High Wycombe, then take the M4 to join the M5 and, eventually, the M6 near to Walsall. At Preston, he spent some time buying a suitable travel case and washing bag. This gave him the opportunity to have a decent meal and buy a litre bottle of Highland Park Single Malt. He also got the largest possible box of expensive chocolates for Anne, and some sweets for the two children, Donald and Margaret. Later on he would stop for flowers to give to Anne.

Due north of Carlisle he took the quieter but pleasanter road to Hawick and, then, across to Kelso. Fortunately, at Hawick, a bouquet of flowers was not forgotten!

The whole family had been on the lookout for him because, on turning into the drive, the two children ran down to meet him. Anne welcomed him with the most affectionate kiss imaginable. David gripped his hand and with his other arm hugged his shoulders.

"Oh!" said Anne, "After all these years it's so wonderful to see you and you look so well. Now, you are here for a wonderful stay for as long as you like!"

"'Hey! You're being far too kind. I'll do my best to live up to your expectations but I'm not the good guy that you think I am! I'm really excited to be able to see you after so many years and, at the same time, to be able to return to Scotland. All this is so exciting."

"I'll be getting a drink poured out for you but please let me show you your room first. You've got the guest room with its own en suite. We've done a lot of alterations since you were last here and you'll find everything very quiet and relaxing." said David. "Oh! By the way. are you still playing golf?"

"No, not for a year or so. Since Madge's death I've sort of lost interest in many of my old activities. Madge was pretty well off after the death of her parents. She invested most of the inheritance and the value of the shares since then has grown. Everything was in my name as well as hers but I'm reluctant to sell anything. For the moment, anyway! But how are you getting on?"

"Well I've been damned lucky. I've had a few promotions recently and the salary that comes with them is doing fine! Oh! Let's go down for a drink. What do you prefer? A dram or two or a gin and tonic?"

"A dram would be great but I'll have a wash first."

Anne was preparing dinner when he came down but a

large dram had been poured for Stan.

Accompanied by Donald and Margaret, Stan followed David into the garden.

"What a terrific garden you've got. You must put a lot of work into it and, gosh, by its looks, you've got a very productive vegetable plot over there! And tomatoes all ready for eating!"

"Yes we've been very lucky with the weather this year. Donald and Margaret are a great help when I am away but. I have to be honest. I've got a gardener who comes in two days a week."

"Dinner's ready." shouted Anne from the doorway.

"We'll have a race to the table!" shouted David, but, inevitably, it was the children who won.

Anne had prepared a most delicious meal. A starter of fresh local salmon followed by the tastiest lamb imaginable, roast potatoes, minted peas and vegetables. For a sweet, there were huge bowls of locally grown strawberries accompanied by fresh cream.

After dinner, the children insisted on playing a few card games but, fortunately, thought Stan, it was not for too long. His travel fatigue was beginning to hit him.

"I've arranged for golf at nine," said David.

"But I've forgotten my clubs," replied Stan in the most apologetic tone he could offer.

"That's OK I've a couple of sets of clubs, with powered trolleys. You can choose tomorrow. Anne has invited several friends for drinks in the evening. I hope you sleep well."

After a marvellous nights sleep, Stan awoke to a glorious

morning of bright sunshine. Although he had not been greatly keen on a game of gold the night before, the sight of the blue skies was beckoning him to come out and enjoy a game. David had already eaten when he went down for breakfast and he was now busily loading his car's boot with the two sets of equipment for the game. Fortunately, he had a spare pair of golf shoes that were ideal for Stan.

Stan's first sight of the course was most rewarding. The colour of the hills and the beauty of the trees were a great background to the splendour of the course and the welcoming look of the greens and the tees. He had a super drive from the first tee and, to his absolute delight, he felt quite heroic when the ball from his second hit made a perfect landing on the par four green.

This was followed by a delightful putt into the hole to give him a most pleasing birdie. He was forced to make light of it to save any embarrassment that David might have when he just managed to sink a bogie. It turned out, though, that this was the pattern for the whole of the game. Stan certainly had his ration of poor drives and putts but this game was sufficient enough to give him a win of five holes.

David reacted by saying, cheerfully. "It must be admitted, I suppose. I have to get the first round of drinks!"

For the evening, Anne had prepared a most attractive display of appetisers and hors d'ouvres. All the families' invited friends confirmed their acceptance of the invitations. David and Anne went out of their way to introduce everyone in a friendly and relaxed fashion. Early on. Stan had noticed the arrival, to him, of a most attractive looking woman. His temperature had risen immediately on seeing her. Anne immediately look his hand and strolled over to greet her.

"Stan, may I introduce you to my best friend, Linda, whom I have had the pleasure of knowing for many years. Linda, Stan is David's cousin."

"Hi! Linda. I've been looking forward tremendously to meeting you. I'm very lucky to have that honour."

"Gosh, Anne! Your relative has the right patter. No! Stan, please forgive me. I have a wicked sense of humour. I, too, am very pleased to meet you."

"I'll leave you both to have a good chat. Please excuse me. I must talk to some of our other friends." said Anne as she moved away.

"Stan, I understand that you have not been here before. Please let me show you some of my favourite views from the garden. If we go through this door here, into the garden, there's a super one by the tree at the end of the lawn. Look, over there towards the hill is my house, which I love dearly. Before he died, my husband made me promise that I would never leave it."

"Yes I can see what a terrific view there is looking over towards it. I suspect you are a great lover of gardens."

'That's Anne ringing her bell to signal that it's eating time. Perhaps after getting something to eat you might like me to show you around. There are so many interesting walks to see."

"I'll not eat much in anticipation!" laughed Stan as they hurried back to the house. The evening continued with much entertainment and joy.

Linda and Stan enjoyed their walk immensely. On

departure, Linda's last words were that she would invite him to see her garden and house within the next few days.

"Come and have a bedtime dram now that the guests have gone." said David.

CHAPTER FIVE

"This is my favourite whisky." said David. "It was very good of you to bring me a bottle of it. I've been drinking it for many years now.

"I know, that's why I bought it."

David looked thoughtful and leaned closer to Stan. "Look, if I appear to be intruding into your private life, please forgive me, but I get the feeling that things are not going too well with you. It may well be that you are still suffering from the loss of Madge, but if this is so, I'll shut up and apologise for intruding into your private thoughts. When we were both young. I was invariably right when I was able to tell that you were cursed by fears known only to yourself."

Stan nodded. "I know, and it was only you who could mind read!" Stan breathed deeply and decided to get it all out. "The truth is that because of my own stupidity I have been dragged into matters that, day by day, appear to become more fearsome than I could ever believe."

"Then please continue."

"You alone are perhaps the only person I feel I can trust and perhaps give me the help I need. It all began by sitting in a pub enjoying a pint of beer when a stranger entered. He offered me another beer which I took and, then, gave me the opportunity to gain £7,000 in return for accepting a sea voyage to the Baltic and then, at Tallinn, making available, to a complete stranger, my persona grata and ship's boarding pass. That person, in looks and dress, would become me and, as such. later enter Britain. Meanwhile with railway and ship tickets, I too, would later enter Dover and proceed to a street convenience where I would receive my £7,000. This is where it gets messy!"

"Gets messy? It already is!"

"Yes, but before I could enter the toilets another guy preceded me. An unknown person then dashed away from the convenience to escape by means of his car parked nearby. I then discovered inside a dead man lying on the floor. Rightly or wrongly I judged it necessary to disappear. It was not until later that I realised that the death blow was meant for me. I should then have notified the police, but I panicked!"

David exhaled. "Oh hell, you have certainly got yourself into a fix, Stan! I can make suggestions to you but, as I see it, there are difficulties lacing you whichever pair you take. Your acceptance of the offer to earn £7,000 could signify you supervising an unlawful immigration into this country. Any claim that this was through naivety is unlikely to be of much help. I have read the national newspapers reporting on the murder but I can't help feeling that there is more to this than meets the eye. If you are prepared to accept the personal dangers likely to be facing you, by admissions to the police, I can have a word with a very close friend in the Metropolitan Police. This could result in a visit to London but you would have to accept the possibility of involvement in legal action. I shall speak to my friend first thing tomorrow if you agree. He will probably want to see you immediately."

"Thanks David. I badly need help even though it could result in future problems. These. I accept."

"OK Stan, I'll let you know tomorrow as early as I can."

Stan had a restless night, lie woke before six and could not get back to sleep. His thoughts were many and varied and always unsettling.

David will do all he can to help but what happens if action is taken against me for committing an immigration offence? After all, his friend is in the police! I have to be honest though, I was tempted by the promise of £7,000 but I was also, rightly or wrongly, influenced by the threat to disclose my misdemeanours of the past!

It was before seven that Stan found himself, fully dressed, walking round the garden. Worried he was, but his desire to walk across to Linda's house was also uppermost in his mind.

Suddenly David appeared in the garden. "All's well Stan. Hector had not left his house before rushing off to work. He would be delighted to see you and, under the circumstances, he suggests seeing you today. He says that there have been more developments since you left London. If you can possibly get an early flight from Edinburgh, he suggests having lunch with you. If you can make the Metropolitan Office and ask for him at reception - Chief Superintendent McDonald - all will be well. He will stay in his office if your flight is delayed."

"Thanks David, I'm not having breakfast but if I go now I might make an early flight!"

He was pleased when he made it to the airport in good time to get a seat, and also to enjoy the on-board breakfast during the short flight to Heathrow. In entering the Met. Office, a messenger took him to Mr McDonald's office, where he was given a most welcoming reception.

"Coffee or tea, Stan? Just call me Hector and hopefully we shall have discussed all the important issues before taking lunch. David, your cousin is a very old friend of mine. He has, I understand, been told of the events experienced by you. On entering Dover you were expecting to receive £7,000. For this purpose, you were told to proceed to a public convenience situated immediately outside the port area. As it turned out an unfortunate guy got there before you and was, there and then, stabbed. On discovering his dead body you left immediately having seen briefly someone else dashing away from the convenience. You would not be able to identify that person. Am I right so far?"

"Yes," said Stan. "It could be, though, that I am unable to offer anything helpful about events that may have happened since."

"Yes, Stan, things have happened since you left but before you leave, later today, I should be most grateful, if you would give me a written statement of all the recent factors, known to you. leading up to the murder. I've decided to update you on subsequent occurrences but you must understand that you are forbidden to tell anyone about what you are about to learn. Before we continue, I must ask you to sign this copy of the Official Secrets Act. If you divulge anything to anyone not authorised, you will be made answerable to a Court of Law. Do you accept this?"

"Yes, I do," said Stan

"Good, Stan. The man who exited the convenience before your entry was subsequently arrested for the offence of exceeding the speed limit both in Dover and on roads outside the town."

"Thank God for that!"

" Indeed. He was later questioned extensively about his current life and activities that might lead to prosecutions for further offences."

"Do you want me to identify him?" offered Stan.

"Ah, bit of a cock up there! He was detained and, incorrectly in my view, before further questioning, allowed a visit by a person other than a Solicitor. The only good factor was that he was secretly photographed prior to seeing the detainee. He spoke to him for several minutes and then, suddenly, asked to leave the police station immediately. Almost instantly after his departure the prisoner collapsed on the floor and died."

"Good God! He must have slipped him poison!"

Hector nodded. "He is currently being examined by Kent's Forensic Pathologist but that's what we believe. He did, however, manage to utter one word - and that was 'Edinburgh,' "

"Hector, many thanks for giving me information which I'm sure is shared by so few. Whilst you have been talking I have been trying to think of anything else which might be helpful. You will see from my statement of events which have taken place, that the person, who now appears to be the leader of others, was at great pains, in weight, looks and dress, to be my double. It is questionable, of course, whether he succeeded in this, but it might be helpful for investigators and others to have an appropriate photograph of me for, hopefully, the purpose of identification. You mentioned specifically the fact that a photograph was taken of the visitor allowed to see the detained prisoner. Would it be possible for me to see that photograph?"

"Yes, certainly. I have a copy in one of my folders. Here it is."

Stan almost jumped with joy. "Yes, yes, it's him. He's the guy who wanted me to travel on a holiday cruise to Tallinn and then make my return trip available to some-one else."

"It's time for lunch Stan but many thanks for the fresh information you have given. It's likely that what you say will be of terrific importance in solving what, at the moment, is a bit of a mystery."

They left the Police headquarters. "My favourite restaurant is along here," said Hector. They have good beer and the food is terrific. Will you have a pint?"

"Nothing better." said Stan.

As they ate. Hector quizzed Stan about his occupa-tion, address and how often he stayed at David's. To his surprise, he asked if he had met Anne's friend Linda. He's very inquisitive, thought Stan, but he told him all he could. On the way back to his office he asked Stan for several photographs to be taken. For this purpose several items of clothing would be made available. Preferably, if it were possible, Stan would dress in the style adopted by the guy at Tallinn. He'd get the official photographer to start as soon as he got back to the office.

Back at the office, Stan decided that something else might be helpful.

"Perhaps you've already given thought to something else where I might be helpful. The Tallinn bloke obviously wanted to enter the U.K., incognito. Hopefully, for this purpose, he decided that a passport was not needed. But it suggests to me that he has most probably been before and. conceivably, is wanted for a previous unlawful act."

"Yes, you are likely to be right there. I'm hoping that your photograph might enable us to identify him from our records and give details of a previous record. This, of course remains to be seen."

"Yes. of course. But if I were to look at all the existing photographs I might, with a lot of luck, find his. After all, I'm the only guy to have seen and spoken to him. Perhaps this is a mad suggestion that might take weeks of search. I am willing to do this!"

"It's certainly not a mad idea. Everything is computerised but if you were successful it would save an enormous amount of manpower research and overtime. I'll discuss this with the Deputy Chief and let you know this afternoon. If he is agreeable, I'll see if accommodation can be found for you. A frequent return journey from the Lothian and Border headquarters is out of the question."

The Chief Superintendent left his office to see if the Deputy would agree. Stan's immediate reaction was to curse himself for volunteering. This would delay getting to know Linda but. at least, he would be able to see her at the weekends. It was with astonishment that, within a few minutes, Hector returned to say that the Deputy Chief had no objections.

"Are you able to start tomorrow Stan?"

After a lot of thought Stan had decided to sell his house in London. This task would give him some time to do so. After all, London prices were very high and a buyer may take a while. Fortunately though, he remembered, just in time, that selling houses necessitated making sellers and buyers aware of a contact address. This might be of help to a prospective killer. He decided to gorget that for a while.

"No problem."

"Great! I'll arrange your hotel right away. With good luck, of course!"

Stan began the following day and to the great surprise of the police office he was able to find, after almost a week, a photo of a certain individual by the name of Mohammed Arqabwi, who was believed to be a member of Al Qua'eda.

In appreciation, John, the photographic officer, and others, arranged a celebratory dinner before Stairs departure.

CHAPTER SIX

It was with great delight that Stan entered the driveway of David's house. His family, with the exception of David, who was away, was delighted to see him.

"Stan, I hope you are feeling hungry. Linda has asked us to her house for dinner this evening. Unfortunately, David can't make it because of being held up in London. He had hoped to be hack in time for the invitation but he's at some business meeting. Never mind. Linda is a wonderful food provider. There will be more for us to eat! Apart from Julius, a neighbour, I don't know who else will be there. I hope none of my patients is invited. Sometimes they can be a menace talking about a damned illness they are loo lazy to come to the clinic about."

"Ah! That's great! I've got my eyes on her. Well I think I have!" laughed Stan.

"She's always been a great friend of mine. Be careful with Julius though. He has a foul temper after a drink or two. If John and his wife Mabel are there, things can be a little heated. John is apt to make fun of him! Anyway, Florie is coming for the night to look after the kids. But how was your trip, I didn't ask?"

"Very busy, I'm afraid. David's friend, Hector Mc-Donald, was very pleasant. He took me out for lunch and later, with some staff, for a dinner."

"You've been lucky. He is a nice chap though. He and his wife stayed with us once for a short holiday. By the way. it's perhaps wiser if we walk to Linda's house. I'm a little fond of wine! But we can go by car if you prefer it?"

"Not at all. Drink is my weakness too!" laughed Stan.

Anne rang the door hell which was answered by Linda.

"Hi Anne. How absolutely terrific that you are both here for dinner and that you, Stan, are able to come. I've got a few friends to join us but I'm sure you'll enjoy their company. What would you like to drink? A dram, gin and tonic, champagne, red or white wine, perhaps... You name it!"

"Thanks Linda, I'd be delighted to have a single malt."

"Ah great! There's a bit of a Scot in you, Stan! Anne, I know your drink, so it wilt be in your hand within a second, but first let me do some introductions at once. Dear friends let me introduce you to David's cousin. Stan. This is Mabel and John, then Jean and Colin, Pauline and Frank and finally, Julius. Excuse me while I dash to bring in some drinks."

"It's Mabel, John. Unfortunately David is away on business but I'm sure that Stan will keep you talking. Now, if you'll excuse me I'll rush off and see what's cooking."

"I see you are staying with Anne and David. What do you think of our part of Scotland. We haven't the wonderful scenery and grandeur of the Highlands but we have the tranquility of the Southern Uplands."

"She's not a Highlander." interrupted Julius. "They're an entirely different race. Friendly, hospitable and nice to know."

"Hell! He's off again. His ancestors were followers of some caliph or other and why not." snarled Curtis.

"Oh dear!" said Frank McDonald as he came over to them. "They're off again. Just patter of course. What's your line of business Stan?"

"Oh, do excuse him!" exclaimed his wife Pauline. "He's inquisitive, to put it politely."

"Well, that's a bit difficult. I've been a Press reporter. Journalist, for a short period, an Actor and a Farmer."

"A farmer, where was that?"

"North Wales." said Stan. "My wife inherited her father's farm and the two of us worked it for several ears."

"Ladies and Gentlemen, dinner is served." said Margaret. Linda's helper, as she entered the room. "Places are all marked."

It turned out to be a most delicious meal. The starter was a salmon and asparagus terrine, followed by a fillet of beef en croute with red wine sauce, roast potatoes and a choice of three further vegetables. The beef was beautifully roasted and completely tender. To Stan's amusement, an argument broke out between Julius and John Curtis as to whether beef should be well cooked or rare. Julius referred to his childhood when any hotel or decent restaurant served beef that was roasted so that the beef was brown in the centre. He could not understand why beef was, according to a modern tendency, oozing with blood in the centre. That was nonsense argued John. Rare meat was always deliciously tender! Anne suggested that they had a vote on the desirability of cooked meal. It was, of course, an overall majority in favour of 'bien cuite' beef. On reflection, though, Stan could not help thinking that it was not very polite for a guest to argue over a host's product. The sweets were terrific; strawberry and cream and/or mango and lime mousse. There was a tremendous choice of wine to accompany the meal.

Of course, the war in Iraq was bound to crop up. The best thing that could happen, in the Middle East, was Julius' theme. The war with Iran, Saddam's atrocities in Northern Iraq, the murder of the river people in Southern Iraq. The many atrocities committed throughout Iraq. The invasion by armed U.S.A. and British forces had been the only solution. These words were enough alone to get John wound up.

"What nonsense. Why should British lives be lost trying to maintain order in a foreign stale. Why should the British taxpayer have to pay for the maintenance of a British army in Iraq?"

Everyone at the table had their own thoughts and, finally, Linda suggested that coffee and drinks should be served in the garden. It was a fine sunny evening and this was an appropriate suggestion. Besides, there were mallets leaning on some of the garden furniture and the loops were set up for an interesting game of croquet. This was a marvellous suggestion. Everyone wanted to play and the game turned out to be an excellent finale to a pleasant evening. Linda and Stan were left when the other guests had left. This provided an opportunity for Stan to say a few words.

"This has been a terrific evening, Linda. The dinner was tremendous and most enjoyable. How would you like to come out to dinner with me, perhaps one evening. Your favourite restaurant would be ideal! Perhaps tomorrow night?"

"That would be great!" laughed Linda.

"I was thinking, wouldn't it be better to go by taxi rather than car? It's so easy these days to be drinking dinner wine and to forget the official driving limit."

"No problem, say six thirty? I'll order the taxi from my home."

"Great! See you tomorrow."

CHAPTER SEVEN

Stan was round at the house a few minutes before the arrival of the taxi. Linda was looking splendid when she opened the front door. She wore an attractive blouse and skirt, both of which so ideally filled her slim and gorgeous figure.

"How beautiful you look!" exclaimed Stan.

"My normal look!" laughed Linda, blushing. "But what about a drink? There's just time before the taxi. A dram suit you?"

"Nothing could be better. I didn't say it yesterday but what beautiful pictures you have."

"Yes. I think they're wonderful. Many of them were inherited. Cheers! Oh, here's the taxi. It's not far to go."

The head waiter was waiting for them when they entered a most sumptuous looking restaurant. He showed them to what could only be described as the most private and attractive table in the room.

"This looks terrific," complimented Stan.

"Oh, it is, and the waiters are all so helpful."

"Are you feeling hungry? The menu has a wonderful selection. What would you like? I've already got my eye on the salmon starter followed by Aberdeen Angus beef-steak."

"Oh, that sounds divine! But I always go for our local river's trout and grouse from our local hills!"

"Great, that's what we'll eat. Now tell me, have you lived here for very long?"

"Oh yes. My parents lived here. Then, when I married, they passed the house over to me. Spoiling me. I think! My husband, Andrew, died here three years ago under tragic circumstances. I still miss him terribly."

"Oh dear! It was about then that I lost my wife. She was a wonderful person. Always the life and soul of a party. She was driving her car one day when an oncoming car, speeding over the 60 mile an hour limit, swerved and hit her head on." He shook his head, sadly.

He continued: "The driver had been drinking but somehow was not badly injured. He got four years for drinking and exceeding the driving limit! I feel he should have got a longer term than that. Madge, my wife, had inherited her father's farm in North Wales, but I sold it on her death and went to live in London. Since then I've done precious little about a future career. May I ask, and please forgive me if it's too presumptuous, but have you been kept busy since your loss?"

"No problem. Yes, I have been kept busy at times helping David. He has, as you probably know, a very tricky job and, at times, I've been away seeking special information for him. I type this and that other material for him. It is of course, very hush-hush and I cannot, I'm afraid, go any further than that."

"Oh! I realise that. I have always known that what he does is highly secretive but I have never once sought any knowledge from him." Stan decided to change the subject. "This red wine is delicious. May I pour out some more of the white wine for you? It still looks cold in the wine bucket."

"Yes, please. How did you manage on your recent trip to London?"

"Fine, I think! They were very pleasant and considerate but I was glad to get away from London. It is, of course, a wonderful city but it's far too crowded for me. Now, what about your sweet? There's quite a choice."

"I think I would like to have the strawberry, cream and meringue Pavlova."

"Great, that's just what I had in mind. After, would you like coffee in the lounge, perhaps followed by a nice liqueur?"

"Yes. please."

Soon, they found nice comfortable arm chairs and enjoyed several more liqueurs.

"Linda, please forgive me if I sound impolite, impulsive, and just sheer mad, but I... I have fallen in love with you. If I were to suggest booking a room in that nice looking hotel across the road, would you be annoyed?"

She was silent for several seconds and then with a large smile said. "Yes, I'd love to. I can now let you into my secret. I've even brought a new toothbrush in my handbag!"

"May I borrow it?"

After a night of splendour, it was a super breakfast and

Stan insisted on having one of the hotel's delicious kippers, followed by wholemeal toast and marmalade. Linda had some work to do at home but she promised to come for a walk on the following day.

It was a lovely morning. The sun shone brightly and Linda was quite happy to walk several miles, after which she suggested that they sat down to admire the view. She was a little puzzled as Stan kept his eyes tied to a particular spot. Finally she asked what was so interesting.

"I don't know. There's a car parked in the small lane over in that direction. I've seen a man move over to the bordering trees. Since then there has been no further movement."

"1 can't see anything, not even the car! Perhaps the poor man needed to relieve himself?"

"What an awful humour you have!" he said, laughing! "I'm just curious. It's too early for blackberries and not a place for mushrooms. I'm going to stand up, hopefully for a better view. You keep seated." Suddenly he shrieked. "Oh Hell, I think it's a Heckler and Koch gun. I thought it was a branch." He fell to the ground, swearing with pain.

Linda stretched out and lay on the ground. She ripped open his shirt and tearing a large section of her blouse, pressed it down on the bullet hole and with the rest of the blouse made a sling for his left arm. "Oh! my God! You're bleeding heavily. You're going to be all right Stan. Please, please, don't leave me."

"I will," sobbed Stan, "if you don't damned well get that flask of whisky I saw you surreptitiously slide into your pocket. Don't get up though, you could easily be the next target." He grabbed the flask and quickly downed as much whisky as he could.

"We'll have to get to Anne quickly. Are we far from her practice?"

"A good distance I'm afraid, but there's a small cottage along the road below. Our gun man has driven away. It will only take me a couple of minutes to run to the cottage and phone Anne. Can you just rest here?"

"I think, darling, I can make it if you can give me support."

"Right Wellington, I'll get you there!"

It turned out to be a hell of a job for Linda but she was determined to succeed and by the time she got to the cottage, both of them were limping badly. Her back was giving her hell! The woman at the cottage was pleased to be of help and within seconds she was through to the practice. Anne was soon available and she immediately arranged for the practice ambulance to be on its way.

"Oh Stan, what on earth has happened? Let me see what I can do! Oh! My God. This is a terrible hole and your shoulder bone is badly damaged. Fortunately, the shot was not low down. It would have been fatal if it had been lower. I'll get through to Edinburgh's Royal as soon as I can. I'll bandage the wound now."

Her limited but tender ministrations over, Anne set about organising everything for Stan's transfer to hospital. She got back to them as soon as she could.

"Our own ambulance, though not as up to date as an

Edinburgh ambulance, will get you there before they get here. I've got Kieran, our emergency driver, to come over straight away, and I've arranged for a District Nurse to go too."

With tears in her eyes Linda looked at Anne to ask if she could possibly go with the ambulance. "Yes. of course! I've got a cup of tea on the way but perhaps a good dram first, might help you to feel a little better. I've also got a spare blouse in the changing room. It should just fit you. I've also spoken to our local police and the headquarters in Edinburgh. A police car has already left to meet our own ambulance in order to supply an escort for the whole of the journey."

"Many thanks Anne. I'd be lost without you. God Bless."

After a thorough examination at the A & E at the Royal, Stan was immediately taken to an operating theatre. A private room was made available for his return. Linda said she was thankful to be able to wait. She was pleased to have the company of a policeman. It had been arranged for him to be part of a permanent guard.

On completion of the operation, Stan was taken to the recovery room. Linda was not allowed to enter but the corridor window of the room was clear enough for her to see Stan asleep.

"Don't worry," said a doctor coming up the corridor. "The bullet has been removed and he should recover satisfactorily. This will take a couple of weeks I'm afraid. You can go into the room as soon as he is awake. I'll get one of the restaurant staff to bring you a drink along. Would you prefer coffee or tea?"

"That's very nice of you. I'd like coffee please, without sugar."

After an hour or so, Stan came to. She rushed inside the room, kissed him and gave him a big hug.

"Darling this is so great to see and speak to you. Are you feeling much pain?"

"None whatsoever but this is probably because of the anaesthetic. As soon as I get out of this hospital I'm going to hunt for the bugger who shot me - he may have hurt you, and I'm not having that!"

"May I come with you?"

"Of course!"

"Good, you can carry the gun and ammunition! Perhaps he hides out on Ben Nevis!"

"That would be a healthy exercise!"

As he was feeling tired, she left him, promising to see him in the morning.

CHAPTER EIGHT

As soon as he was able David went to visit Stan in hospital. He was anxious to see if Stan could throw further light on the attempt to kill him. Stan was beginning to recover from the serious wound in his shoulder and now was the time, he thought, to determine exactly why he was considered a threat to whatever organisation was seeking an apparent threat to Britain.

"Great to see that you are beginning to recover, Stan. All this must be a bloody trial for you."

"Well if you put it like that, it is a bit frightening but I'm determined to get better and see if I can be of some help. Lying here I've been trying to work out why I'm worth killing. Then there was the prisoner who died in Dover. He was allowed a visitor that, considering the early stage of his imprisonment, was bloody stupid. Why is it that the one and only word uttered by the guy dying in Dover was 'Edinburgh'? Was this in revenge for being poisoned by his own people and was it an indication that Edinburgh was the target for some drastic action?"

"Yes, I think after your conversation with Chief Superintendent McDonald, I can now be pretty open about the whole damned thing. There is no news, as yet, about the pathologist's analysis but others have similar thoughts to yours, but there are other things puzzling me. Why is there an apparent desire to kill you and how, in the whole of Britain, were you identified or known to be in Kelso?"

"I'm very puzzled too. Admittedly. Linda and I, after drinking and eating in two separate places, were seen by others. Putting aside the photographs taken of me sitting in the pub in London, there are only two people who would recognise me and they are the two *I* met in connection with my trip to Tallinn."

"Aye. you are right here but the photos can be an enormous lend for a lot of people. but I think your thoughts on the mention of 'Edinburgh' are the best yet. I intend getting a meeting in Edinburgh organised. The dreadful bomb killings in London could be an indication of possible occurrences in other parts of Britain. The war in Iraq has increased the terrorist threat to Britain, there's no doubt about that. A report from the Royal Institute for International Affairs says that the invasion gave a lift to al Qua'eda's recruitment and that, as a result, there were 'particular difficulties for the U.K.' In Scotland alone, Edinburgh, and for that matter Glasgow, Dundee and Aberdeen are under possible threat - utilising all our Police Forces and Intelligence Agencies does not mean we can sit back under the assumption that all will be well."

"Dave, I find that lying in bed in hospital produces the most absurd thoughts in one's mind. Some of them are completely mad. Certainly the use of explosives or bombs is uppermost but although such chemicals as acetone peroxide are not difficult to use, despite the occurrence in manufacture of death to the maker, it may be, for the killer, easier to use other products. I'm thinking here of a mass use of poison."

"Poison? Horrible!"

"A poison which, for its use. does not necessarily require a vast quantity. The swift death of the detainee in Dover's Police Station points to the possibility of a use of a poison and, here, you will possibly know something from the post-mortem examination. But, I should imagine, the difficulty with a poison for a mass destruction of humans is in its appliance and distribution. Who would consume the product containing the substance before it was discovered? In a manufacturing process, who would have the capability to include it as a component of the final product? Here, not without horror, I have thought of Scotland's production of whisky. The final step in its manufacture is that in the bottling hall. The blend, perhaps of several whiskies or of a single malt."

"Your commendable theories on this subject will be given a thorough examination. I'm afraid that I have to rush now but you'll be pleased to know that Linda is about to see you. I've just spotted her through the window. Make sure that you always have a policeman in the corridor outside your door. Bye!"

"Hi love. How nice to see you. I'm a lucky guy."

"Of course you are. Are you improving? Less pain, I hope."

"Yes but I'm getting fed up being tied to this room even though I have a T.V."

"Never mind, here's a nice kiss and a hug!"

"Can't you stop the night?"

"I might get shot!"

"No, that's for me."

"Any news?" I've just seen David leaving but he was in a hurry and hadn't much to say. I've not heard anything but I miss you tremendously."

"Linda, I get terribly bored lying here and I keep trying to analyse everything and, although I can recognise why I could be a threat to the Tallinn guy, how did they find out that I was in Kelso?"

"I've tried too! There are no new people here apart from a few holiday visitors."

"It may sound a little odd but I've been giving a lot of thought to your dinner party guests. The liveliest at the table were Julius and John Curtis. They seemed very nice people but I wondered at times if their banter was just an act. If it were an act, it was a damned good one. Were they disguising a hatred for each other and. if so, what was the cause of it?"

"They have always been like that. John has been here for a great number of years and his wife, Mabel, is a very nice person. Julius has only been here for a couple of years. He's a lively sort of person and is well known in the town. Strangely enough, I don't know anything about his origins. He goes overseas quite a lot but I know nothing about his career. I've always assumed that he is single but have never really known. I do know though, that he can speak a few languages."

"He's dark skinned, could he originate in the Middle East?"

"Yes, I think he could. Incidentally, I have not seen him for a couple of days."

"What about John Curtis? Does he go away often?"

"I don't really know but I would think no more than for annual holidays."

"As soon as I can leave the hospital I'm going to do some research, although I'm not too sure what the result will be!"

"Can I come?"

"Of course! There will be no fee! I wonder though, as a start, if it's possible to find out if Julius has any mail from the Middle East. Does he have a house cleaner? I would like to be able to look around his house."

"For a gun?"

"Oh yes!"

"Do you think he shot you?"

"Possibly."

"Would you shoot him?"

"Yes, but I'd aim for his shoulder!"

"Would you miss?"

"Possibly!"

"Well I'd better go now. I've got some shopping to do. Bye my love, I'll see you tomorrow."

CHAPTER NINE

After doing some shopping. Linda got in her car and drove southward. She wanted so desperately to be able to help Stan. Then, it came to her - why not break into Julius's house herself. If he were away this would be an ideal time. If he came back suddenly and she was in the house she could perhaps make some excuse. After all, she had been trained in self defence and Julius wasn't exactly a strong looking guy. Now, what would she need for a break in? Two screwdrivers, a Phillips and a normal one, a light hammer and, of course, her equipment for mastering locks, provided to her when she was under training at the M.O.D. Special Studies Group.

This is exciting, she thought, as her gadget for entry began to turn. The door pushed silently open. *No, this is hugely exciting!*

The entrance hall was spotlessly clean but how odd. She had been told by the Post Office that he was away but there were no letters lying in the post box. It must have been the cleaner taking them to Julius's study. With enthusiasm she started a room by room search. Then, to her horror, she heard the lock of the front door being manipulated in the same fashion that she had carried out.

With horror she looked desperately around the study for a place of refuge. It was not a big room but, in the comer, was a door, perhaps leading into another room. It was not locked but it turned out to be just a large cupboard but thankfully with sufficient room to hide. Julius was entering the room. He seemed to be walking slowly towards the cupboard door. A hand was on the door-knob.

"Ha! Ha! My dear hide-a-way. What have we got here? A lodger, perhaps!" said John Curtis.

"Ah! It's you, John. Julius said I could borrow a book for some research!"

"Did he now! In a cupboard? In the dark? And why did you spend some time fiddling with the front door lock?"

"Em, the lock needed some oil to help it on its way – but what the hell are you doing here?"

"Julius asked me to look after his house. But now you are going to come with me. Your fine little romance with Stan is about to end."

"Oh no it isn't!" cried Linda as she lifted her foot to kick him in the crutch. But she was too late. He quickly side stepped, stooped, and, with his right hand, grasped her ankle. With a simple jerk upwards she found herself flying downwards, her head striking the door jamb.

Very faintly she heard Curtis shout, "Now you'll have to learn how to behave!"

It was some time before she came to, and when she did there was a slight throbbing in her head. To her astonishment, she found that her hands were bound together but, to her horror, she discovered that her ankles were also tied.

"What the hell is all this," she said out loud. She was lying stretched out on the back seat of a car. She could just make out that John Curtis was driving.

"John what on earth are you doing? We've been friends for years and many a time you've dined at my house. You were also a great friend of my late husband."

"Yes, Linda, I'm extremely sorry about all this but you've left me with no alternative. There's is a danger for me that you are about to disrupt my life. This would never have happened if you had not taken up with Stan Watson. He is a great danger to me and my associates. He has to be removed. I'm sorry about the distress this is going to cause you."

"You bastard! It was you who shot him?"

"Yes."

"But you only managed to wound him in the shoulder."

"Unfortunately. But you are forcing me to ensure that this is never known to others in Kelso. I and others have yet to decide what is going to happen to you. I dare say you won't be executed. But you'll he kept as a prisoner – for a long time. There is no other alternative!"

"You're an absolute bastard. Curtis! I'll make sure that you'll never succeed."

Silence reigned in the car until they arrived in Edinburgh. As far as Linda could ascertain, they stopped in front of a garden flat in New Town.

A man and woman appeared outside the car and with a stretcher carried Linda down the steps and into the flat.

Without a word, Curtis drove away.

Linda was taken to a door in the corridor. She was taken into the room.

"This will be your home." said the woman. "This is a bedroom and the door to the left will take you to your bathroom. You will be given food each day and I shall provide you with soap. If you don't cause trouble I shall try to get you a T.V. For the moment, you will be chained to the end of the bed. Hammer on the door if you desperately need anything but don't forget you are here as a prisoner."

No, no, said Linda to herself. *Think what you like but I shall escape.* She lay down on the bed and was soon asleep.

CHAPTER TEN

The sun was shining brightly and brilliantly beaming into Stan's room. He felt great and could not feel any pain in his shoulder. Linda had promised to see him that morning and, hopefully, she was leaving her home early. Maybe he could leave the hospital that day and return to the glorious life he was having at her home. His pleasant thoughts continued until his breakfast was brought in. It would not be long before she entered the room.

The hospital routine was now underway but apart from medical staff entering the room, there was no sign of Linda. Maybe the traffic had been held up. Sometimes there were delays. But it would soon be lunchtime. She would have phoned by now. Oh hell, could something serious have happened? It was time for him to do some phoning.

"Hello Anne. It's me, Stan."

"Hi Stan! Are you feeling better? I'm sorry I've not been able to come to Edinburgh but I did not want to leave the kids. Linda has phoned me daily except for yesterday. I was going to phone you later. I thought that perhaps she was staying over in Edinburgh but when I went to the practice, I noticed that her car was stationed in her drive.

I should have phoned you but I've been tied up with patients this morning."

"Oh help! Anne. She always comes early and phones if there is a reason for the delay. I'm sure now that something drastic has happened. Can David help, do you think?"

"He's in London. He said he didn't know when he would be back."

"Right. I'm coming back. I don't know if the consultant will say it's okay but I'm frightened that something serious has happened, He's just on his rounds. Oh, can you hold on for a second or two? He's just come into the room."

Stan addressed the consultant. "Mr McDonald, my lady friend who was supposed to see me this morning has disappeared. You've met her and you will recall that she was with me when I was shot. I feel desperate and I must have your agreement that I leave the hospital."

"Well, I can see that you have one hell of a problem. I'll be honest. My professional opinion is that you stay for at least another two days, but I suspect that you will go despite what I say. So if you promise to continue to wear the sling, to rest a lot, and not travel far from your home, I agree."

"Ah! That's great. Thanks very much for your help. I'll drive slowly."

"Anne I'm sorry to keep you waiting but my consultant has agreed, not without some displeasure, though. I'll just have to take things easily. But I'm worried stiff."

"I'll look after you, Stan, don't worry. From what you

say I think it is essential that you come back to your room here. It's nice and quiet and you can rest whenever you feel like it."

"That's truly kind of you Anne. I'm absolutely delighted by your offer and I hope that I'll not be too much of a worry about Linda."

"No problem Stan. I look forward to seeing you."

CHAPTER ELEVEN

Stan had a pleasant albeit tiring journey hack to Kelso, but he was determined to start his enquiries as soon as possible. His first visit was to the Police Station, where Inspector McDougal promised to make any enquiry possible. He reminded Stanley not to lose sight of the fact that he was, probably, still a target. He also told him to be very careful of others. Someone, possibly from Kelso, was trying to kill him.

Stan's next port of call was at Julius's house. He had not expected to see his car standing outside the front door of Julius's house. Julius came to the door when he rang.

"Hello Stan! How nice to see you. I hope you are feeling better. Please come inside."

"Thanks Julius. I'm just paying a visit to all of Linda's friends. She was due to visit me yesterday in the Royal Hospital in Edinburgh but she never arrived and I don't seem able to contact her."

"Oh, God!"

"Have you any idea where she might be found?"

"No, I'm sorry. It's terrible about her disappearance. I've been away and this is the first time I've heard that you are looking for her. Perhaps we can talk further about this. But first, would you like a whisky or perhaps a sherry or a coffee?"

"I've not been taking alcohol whilst I've been in hospital but I should be pleased to take a sherry."

"Right, if you'll excuse me I'll get some."

This pleased Stan because whilst they had been talking he had noticed a button to a lady's blouse which was lying on the floor near to a door at the far corner of the room. He quickly ran across the room and pocketed it. He examined it closely and was pretty certain that it belonged to the blouse worn by Linda on her last day of seeing him in hospital.

Julius arrived back in the room with sweet and dry bottles of sherry, together with some extremely expensive looking wine glasses.

"Have you been away for long Julius?" said Stanley to put him quickly on the defensive. "And how's business?"

"Just short of a week all together. I've been to Beirut this time. As regards business, it's growing like mad and I've been trying to assess what products are likely, when imported, to be the most advantageous to the British exporter. Returning to Linda, from what you say I'm very concerned about the difficulties you are having finding her. She is a lovely person and I have a great regard for her. Have you got in touch with police to see if they can help?"

"Yes, as a matter of fact I have. I have the dreadful feeling that she has not gone away under her own volition. Someone has perhaps kidnapped her deliberately. Who knows, perhaps there is a connection with the mystery man who tried to kill me."

"That really was terrible. I was away at the time and so did not hear of the terrible news until I returned. You must have some thoughts as to why someone sought your death?"

"I think one would have to be very daft not to search one's past for clues as to why there was a wish for my death. I have not been able to find an answer. Perhaps we could have another talk on this subject. I must now go but thank you very much for the delightful sherry."

Now I must have a talk with John Curtis. Better late than never, thought Stan. To his surprise John's car, just like that of Julius's, was standing at the front of his house.

"Hello Stan, nice to see you. Please come in. Are you feeling better? Your stay in hospital cannot have been too pleasant."

"Yes, the stay had its moments of pain. I wish I could get hold of the bugger who tried to kill me. It was very mysterious. Who do you think could do such a thing?"

"I haven't a clue." was the abrupt reply.

"I was thinking of the Territorial Army or even National Service?"

"Oh come on! I'm not old enough to have done National Service."

"No, of course not! Have you seen anything of Linda? She never came to see me the whole of the time that I was in hospital. I wonder why?"

"Oh! I heard from local gossip that she visited you often."

"Sheer gossip, I suppose. I understand that you know Scotland extremely well. Have you any suggestions where I might find her?"

"I don't think I can help you there. She could be anywhere. She's a very intelligent person. Perhaps she will turn up."

"Are you still in business, John?"

"I never discuss my business."

"Sorry. I was thinking that if your business involved a lot of travel, you might have some idea where she is?"

"None whatsoever."

"But you've known her for many years. You also knew her husband. Perhaps you can recollect a place which they visited often because they loved it so much?"

"Look, you've asked so many questions. I've had enough and I don't want any more."

"What about Mabel? She's a friend. Perhaps she would help?"

"No, she wouldn't."

"Right, I must go John. Our conversation has been interesting." said Stan in a sarcastic tone.

CHAPTER TWELVE

Linda awoke early in the morning. Although the room appeared miserable and completely odd, it did not take her long to realise that she was imprisoned in one of New Town's below ground level flats. She noticed that a large area of one of the walls had been boarded up at some time. It had been done very badly by an obvious amateur.

Morning light was already showing in the gaps between the boards screwed into the wall. It was now fairly obvious that there was a window behind the board. It could be facing a road, from which stone steps descended to the front door to the flat. The alternative to this would be that it was overlooking a garden at a level below the window. On leaving her home to search Julius's house and that of John Curtis she had changed into a pair of slacks with two large pockets. Nobody had subsequently searched her and she could still feel the two screwdrivers together with a small hammer and a gadget to pick the lock. She hurriedly placed the tools below the bed's mattress.

The chain attached to the end of the iron bed was long enough to enable her to reach the wood concealing the window. Although the room was dimly illuminated, there was sufficient light to enable her to identify the holes of the screws anchoring the board to the wall. She lay for some time longer, firmly fixing their position so that, as soon as night fell, she could, by touch, begin to work on her escape route.

It seemed to her an enormously long day. The food for her meals was dismal and her gaolers scarcely uttered a word. The ceiling lights were controlled from outside the room and reading a book was a great strain. She was able, however, to spend some time examining her chain's attachment to the bottom of the bed. The fastening was merely achieved by screws and nuts. They would not be much of a problem and to prove this, she loosened the screws to enable further progress to be done by hand.

At long last supper came, frugal and stale. Later still, the ceiling lights were switched off. She was shaking with excitement. She *was* going to succeed. The removal of the chain was the first success, followed, perhaps, by the boards. All she needed was sufficient room for her to have access to the window locks. This part of the process did not lake long and to her surprise the window was secured by nothing more than the latches either side of the sash windows. She gathered the meagre items that she had brought with her and squeezed through the window to be able to slide to the slab below. She was at the front of the house and it only took seconds to be in a position to be able to run full speed down the road.

She now had to decide fairly quickly what to do. If she went to the Royal Hospital, Stan might have left it and gone back to Kelso. To join him there she could run to the bus station but the plain truth was that she was completely penniless and unable to buy a ticket. She had but one option and that was to get to a police station as soon as possible. As far as she knew 'The West End' was the nearest but she had to be very careful. Her gaolers and others might already be dashing around by car searching for her. Suddenly, and to her surprise, she saw a police car driving towards her. She stepped into the road and waved for it to stop which it did immediately. One of them said that he knew about the attempt to kill Stan but, in his own words, said that the "high hied yins" were looking into it.

It was a duty Superintendent that she saw. He said that he knew Stan was back in Kelso because he'd called on Inspector McDougal as soon as he got there.

"I'm really excited to hear that he has made Kelso safely. I'm terribly worried about him. For the moment though. I believe the best thing to do is if I tell you about my breaking into an acquaintance's house in Kelso to see if I could find any evidence of those wishing to kill him."

She sighed, then continued. "This visit was not successful because I had no sooner started looking when another acquaintance, named John Curtis, succeeded in breaking into the house. He, too, was an old friend, living in Kelso, who had frequently had meals at my house. I went into hiding but it did not take long for him to find me. He attacked me. I lost consciousness. It was not until I was halfway to Edinburgh that I realised that my hands and feet were tied and that I was lying on the back seat of his car. He told me that I would be held prisoner in a flat in The New Town. From what he said, his mission was to kill Stan as soon as he could. In fact, it was he who had fired at him for that very purpose."

"It is most likely that, given the time, you will be able to tell me a lot more but, for the moment. I think it is imperative for immediate action to be taken. I'll speak to Inspector McDougal immediately if I'm able to contact him. Stan will need a permanent guard and Curtis must be arrested immediately. I'll also arrange for Inspector Mitchell to arrest the people who had you in custody. This, also, will be done immediately. If you have no objection, may I ask you to accompany him and the constables who will do the arrest?"

"Nothing will give me greater pleasure!"

"Correct me if I'm wrong, but I suspect that you are not able to give the number of the house and the name of the road?"

"You are absolutely right."

Fortunately, Linda recognised the flat of her imprisonment immediately. Her keepers were both asleep even though there was little quietness during the police entrance. She and the police were delighted because the possibility of Curtis being informed was now out of the question. Unfortunately, Curtis was not found in the town or surrounding countryside of Kelso which meant, of course, that the greatest care must be continued to ensure their survival.

"Mr. McGruther, you are now in an interview room. Everything that is said in this room will be recorded. I am turning on the recorder now. I have to warn you that anything you say may be taken down and may be given in evidence at your trial in a Court of Law. You have been introduced to Mr Grant sitting next to you. He will act as your legal representative and if you are in doubt about anything said, he is there to advise you. I am Inspector Mitchell and the policeman on my right is Sergeant Hawkins. Today is the 19th of September 2005 and the time is nine thirty in the morning. You were arrested yesterday evening because you had been holding Mrs Linda Sutton, against her will, in a room set aside for that purpose. Was there a lock on the door to the room?"

"No, of course not. Mrs Sutton was able to come and go as she pleased."

"Was the light switch to the room within the room?"

"No, for some reason or other the electrician had put the switch in the corridor outside the room."

"Was Mrs Sutton able to switch the light on inside the room?"

"No, but all she had to do was to go into the corridor to switch it on."

"Was Mrs Sutton imprisoned by a chain, the end of which was anchored to the bed?"

"No. I know of no chain."

"How do you account for the fact that one of Mrs Sutton's ankles was found to be badly bruised. On our arrival at your basement flat, a chain attached to one of the legs of the bed was found lying on the floor. The ring at the other end of the chain securing Mrs Sutton's ankle had been unscrewed. The relative screws and nuts were found to be lying on the floor."

"I know nothing about this."

"So where did the chain come from?"

"Mrs Sutton must have brought it with her."

"But the chain was screwed to the end of the bed. Was she carrying the bed on her arrival?"

"No, of course not!"

"Now tell me, Mr McGruther, Mrs Sutton arrived in a car driven by Mr John Curtis. Her wrists were bound together and her ankles were also tied. Did you help her get out of the car and into your flat?"

"Yes."

"But her wrists and ankles were bound."

"Well, I carried her."

"What! Down the narrow steps from the road pavement into the basement flat?"

"No! Marion helped me."

"Marion, who lives with you?"'

"Yes."

"So there were three of you together on the sleep narrow step; you, Mrs Sutton and Marion? The wrists and ankles of Mrs Sutton were bound. Was Marion in front of you or behind you?"

It went on like this for ages, the police lobbing questions, the prisoner fobbing them off, until he finally cracked under the pressure.

"Ah! Bloody, bloody hell! I've had enough of this. She arrived at the back of Mr Curtis's car. Her wrist and ankles were tied. Marion and I carried her on a stretcher into the flat."

"Then into the room and YOU shackled one of her ankles to the bed?"

"Yes."

'What was Mr Curtis doing all this time?"

"He never left the car. He pelted away as soon as we got her out of the car."

"Whom do you work for?"

"How do you mean?"

"Who pays your wages?"

"I get money sent to me each month."

"For what?"

"Looking after the basement flat."

"How is the money sent to you?"

"It's dropped through the letter box in the door."

"Payment by cheque, money order, or postal order?"

"The notes come in a large envelope."

"Are you given instructions in the envelope?"

"Sometimes."

"To do what?"

"It varies. Delivering instructions to certain people or to prepare sleeping arrangements for guests."

"What happens to the instructions?"

"I have, at once, to burn them."

"Returning to the people who give you jobs to do. What is the name of their organisation?"

"I don't know. I've never met them. Mr Curtis is the only person I've met."

"Do you have any telephone numbers other than Mr Curtis's number?"

"No."

"Mr. McGruther, it is now eleven fifteen and the end of my questions. You will now be taken back to your cell."

Inspector Mitchell left the room to speak to Superintendent Harding. He told him about the success of McGruther's interview where he finally confessed to imprisoning Linda but was unable to give any information about the organisation employing him.

"Fortunately," he said, "he was open about Curtis who appeared to be the only known person of the existing organisation. Sergeant McMillan had done extremely well in her questioning of the woman known as Marion. There was a complete confession of responsibility for Linda's treatment but she tried to transfer the whole blame on to the shoulders of McGruther."

"I'm very pleased. This has been a most successful operation and I'm delighted by the performance of everyone concerned. We must not lose sight, however, of the importance of learning about the background to the offences that have already taken place. I am still convinced that Stan Watson and Linda remain at the top of the list for murder. Stan was at the beginning with his trip to Tallinn. It has to be that, because he alone could immediately recognise the apparent leaders of whatever organisation exists, he must be destroyed. Both of them must now have protective guards for their survival. It is absolutely vital that there is an immediate arrest of this crook, Curtis."

CHAPTER THIRTEEN

Linda was madly excited. She was going home to see Stan. Her car was still in Kelso but Detective Superintendent Harding had very kindly arranged for a police car to take her back home. He had also come to her rescue by loaning her some money to rush out and buy some new clothes in order that she could be wearing something nice for Stan to see her at her best. Sergeant McMillan had been very helpful too. She'd made arrangements with her hairdresser for an immediate and glamorous treatment of her hair. This had been done early in the morning and her blonde hair now looked, both in shape and colour, as elegant as any woman could wish. "Bloody marvellous!" said one of the admiring policemen as she re-entered the police station. Another one said that the whole station would be wanting to see her in court when she appeared as a prosecuting witness against McGruther!

To be honest, she had suffered excessively, brief though it was, in her imprisonment in the basement flat. She had succeeded in escaping, but in so doing she had gone through hell; but, being the sort of woman that she was, she had outwardly suppressed any sign of self pity. Her greatest concern had been and would continue to be the shooting of Stan, by, in her own words, "Curtis, the absolute bastard". Now, however, was one of the greatest times of her life. She was free and going home. She was going home to Stan.

"Mrs Sutton." said D.C.S. Harding's Secretary as she approached. "Your driver is at the front of the building waiting to take you home. Detective Constable Derek Holm will also be the guy who will net as the protector of both you and Mr Watson. He is a nice guy and is very popular in the station here. He will be armed all the time and, in fact, is a most excellent shot. May I wish you the very best wishes for the future."

"Thank you very much. You and the rest of the station have been most kind. Bye."

It was now raining and she ran to the ear. Her luggage, small that it was, had already been placed in the boot.

"Hi, Mrs Sutton! I'm here to look after you. My name is Derek Holm. I will not be in uniform – in fact, I've left it at home. I'm armed to protect you and Mr Watson at all times. If you need any help whatsoever, please just give me a shout."

"Thank you very much, Derek. Might I say that Stan and I are very glad, after our respective experiences, to have you with us. Please let me know what your favourite meals are and let me know what you dislike. We have a ground floor, with bedroom and bathroom. Would you be happy sleeping there?"

"Yes. It would be ideal. It's much better to have a downstairs room because most house break-ins occur at that level. I must confess that I have never been to Kelso before. Perhaps you can keep me on the best road?"

"No problem! After leaving Edinburgh, you come into very nice country. Where in Scotland do you come from?"

"'My early days were spent at Tomatin. My father was the Excise Officer there so I have a good knowledge of how to make a Highland Malt! I had three brothers so I also had a marvellous training in deer stalking and fishing salmon! Rightly or wrongly, I chose the Police Force rather than the Excise. I've been with the Police for three and a half years now and I'm hoping to be offered a place soon at Scotland's Police College."

Jokingly, she said, "Are you good at shooting?"

Realising that there was an element of humour behind this question he said: "Oh yes, at the age of fourteen I won an international adult competition for shooting deer!"

Linda now felt herself completely at ease with her future lodger as she pointed out places of interest. She felt that Stan would have similar thoughts to hers.

At last they drove into the drive of her house. Stan came rushing out. Oh! It was so wonderful to see him. He came racing out and threw his arms around her.

"Oh Linda! It's so terrific seeing you. I've been so worried about you and I love you so much. When can we get married? Soon I hope. Oh! You look so wonderful. Your hair, your face, your clothes and the whole of you is tremendous."

He lifted her into his arms and carried her into the house. She held on to him tightly and with tears in her eyes, she said: "Oh! Stan, my love for you is so great. I've been through hell worrying about you and praying that you are recovering. It has been a sheer misery without you. Yes! Lei's get married as soon as we can get rid of this monster Curtis and his gang! Heck, Stan, I've completely forgotten about Derek. He's standing outside in the rain wondering what to do."

"Who on earth is Derek?"

"He's now our protector, specially selected by the police to look after us. He's also a champion shot! You'll like him. I'm putting him in the ground floor bedroom and I'm just waiting for him to shoot Curtis!"

"Okay, lei's grab him before he gets soaked in the rain and is completely disillusioned about us. I'll pick up his luggage."

Stan ran as fast as he could to get to Derek before he retreated back into his car for shelter. He grasped his hand firmly.

"Hi Derek. I'm sorry for leaving you here in the rain but it's a pleasure to welcome you now. Very many thanks for bringing Linda safely home. I hope you'll be happy living here with us."

"It'll be great, sir. I've never been to Kelso before or, in fact, any of the country around here. Mrs Sutton has had a good journey home and seems to be recovering very quickly from her awful experience. Is your shoulder a lot better, sir?"

"It's fine now Derek, but I'd feel a hell of a lot better if you'd call me Stan! I don't think I've ever been ad-dressed as 'sir'."

"Sorry. I'm so used to calling people 'sir' that it takes

quite a while not to do it. I'm hoping to be able to look after you well and to keep Curtis well away."

"Don't worry! I've already thought that it would be fun to call you 'sir' every time you call me it! Let's show you your room."

"Linda" he shouted, "is everything ready for Derek?"

"Yes, I've even laid out towels in the bathroom and a box of chocolates on the bedside table!"

Looking embarrassed, Derek said, "That'll be great Mrs Sutton but before I settle in, I should be very grateful if you could show me all the rooms upstairs together with their windows; followed by those downstairs and all the doors of entry to the house. If there is an attic, I should like to look around that as well. Also the garage and any out houses. After that I would like to look around the garden and the immediate neighbourhood."

"No problem, I'll show you upstairs and Stan will give you a tour of downstairs and the gardens." With a broad grin she also added, "Perhaps you could let me know if you have any likes or dislikes in food."

With an equal grin, he replied, "I love all food!"

After giving him a full tour of upstairs, Linda handed him over to Stan. As requested, Stan showed him all the areas that might give shelter to anyone attempting to use a gun or a weapon designed to kill.

"I'll show you a far wider area as soon as you are ready but perhaps you'd like to join us for a meal before-hand?"

"Yes. That'll be great."

"Do you prefer white or red wine?"

"Oh! I'm sorry, I never take alcohol of any descriptions whilst I'm on duty."

"That's okay, as long as you don't mind us drinking?"

"Like hell!"

"Well, as soon as you clean the countryside of any threat, I'm taking you out for a superb dinner with as much drink as you can knock back."

Derek reached for his notebook hidden away in his back pocket and said,

"I'm writing down what you have just said. Failure to comply with what you've said might result in your immediate arrest!"

With an outburst of delighted laughter. Stan muttered, "Aye, aye, sir. We should now visit Linda for some grub."

After an enormous feast, Derek telephoned the Kelso police station to advise them of his presence. Inspector McDougal gave him his home telephone number and said that he would arrange with British Telecom for a special emergency line from the station to Mrs Sutton's house. He would also arrange for two Constables to be on duty during the night hours. The emergency code word would be 'protection'.

After instructing Stan to lock even door and window in his absence, Derek made another survey of the garden and surroundings. Finally, in his ear, he paid a quick visit to Curtis's house and that of Julius's. On return, he would make a point of asking Linda for the surname of the latter.

Before retiring. Derek reminded Linda and Stan that

if there were a caller, perhaps saying that they had arrived with an order, it should be viewed through a window with the door closed. If necessary, the supplier of the item should be telephoned for confirmation. If it were then claimed not to have been ordered by them personally, they should know immediately that they were under siege. They should contact him immediately and. if necessary, 'phone the police station.

CHAPTER FOURTEEN

He had been extremely careful in disguising his real name originating in the Middle East and in the use of the several European names he had adopted. Though, as regards the latter, the British names he found were usually the easier to assume. He could, quite easily call himself Abdullah Mohammed or Donald Smith and, from his conversational ability, it might take an expert linguist days of study to determine the true tongue of his birth.

He was also adept at adopting the proper mannerisms belonging to the language he was using. Despite these assets he would take endless trouble in protecting the validity of the person he was representing. He had, for instance, chosen a short residence in Tallinn to be able to secure secrecy in the travel to and entry into the United Kingdom. He had entered this country to cause havoc but, because of events of which he had no control over, he had to revise, perhaps, the whole of his plans. He had in the recent past set up several organisations to assist in the success of what he thought would be worthy achievements. His own employees had. through negligence, caused the death of two individuals. Another agency, of unknown, but possibly Al Qua'ida magnitude, had put into action the massacre of ordinary innocent London people. The reaction to the latter had been the creation of a more energetic and protective police force designed to bring to justice those responsible. Any action that he had conceived must now take place in a city or area far north of London. He was now resident in Edinburgh. This gave him greater scope for his northern plans. He was convinced, however, that what he did would be a great success.

For the moment he had two problems that had to be resolved. This man, Watson; and now the woman, Sutton. They knew too much about his existence. Curtis, who had been over the years a most useful member of his organisation, was now making mistakes. His usefulness was now at the edges, wearing thin. Once again he must demonstrate his worth.

"Kaleem," he shouted to his assistant, "would you get Curtis to see me immediately."

Curtis did not lodge far away and it was only a few minutes before he was knocking at his boss's door.

"Enter." shouted Abdullah. "Are you making good progress?"

"Yes, Sir!"

"So you have annihilated Watson and Sutton?"

"No, not quite, Sir. I am planning within the next day or two to return to Kelso and, with the assistance of two of our team, kill them immediately."

"Good! Now, what are your proposals for the future?"

"It would be unwise, at this time, to return to the south of England. Edinburgh, Glasgow, Aberdeen and Dundee are ideal targets for bombs or explosions but I feel that we must not rush before making a thorough survey. There is, of course, also the possibility of using poisons."

"Report back to me soon."

Having worked many years for Mohammed, Curtis was well aware that he had just been censured. Against this, he was able to recognise that he was paid extremely well and, over time, he had amassed enormous sums in banks throughout the world. At first he had found it exceedingly wicked to kill other human beings and against all principles of decent, let alone, holy living. Army service had eventually hardened him and perhaps adjusted him to the horror of killing others. Fortunately, in modem times, such an adherence, certainly in western society, was on the decline.

After a couple of days' preparation he set out to return to Kelso. He had chosen Kahmed and Aliyah,, both members of Mohammed's cell, to assist him. They were to go to a furniture store in Coldstream and buy an upholstered couch. To cover the delivery of the van and content to Kelso and back to Coldstream they were to provide a generous deposit. At the appropriate address to be told to them, they were to carry the couch to the front door and in response to the opening of the door, they were to shoot dead the persons standing before them. The same treatment was to be given to other people standing in the doorway. Whilst the commotion was taking place at the front door, Curtis, who had established himself at the back of the house, would break a window and enter the house. He would proceed to the front and shoot dead any of the house occupants.

CHAPTER FIFTEEN

Two men entered the furniture shop in the town of Coldstream. They looked as though they were possibly from the Middle East. They appeared a little lost as they wandered around the shop. "Can I help you?" said Ian Macduff who was standing at the counter.

"I am looking for a sofa." explained the taller one.

"No," said the other, "it is a settee."

"You mean a couch," said Ian

"No, a sofa." muttered the taller.

"No, a settee." retorted the smaller.

"Okay." replied Ian, pulling two fingers to his lips as a signal to his lady assistant who was now near hysterical. "The couches are in the back room. My assistant will show them to you."

After a further debate, the customers chose a blue two-seater. They then paid for it and asked if they could rent a van to carry the couch to Kelso. They would return the van after delivery. Finally, after securing a good rental price, Ian agreed.

"Please," uttered the taller, "it is to be delivered to a Mrs Sutton in Kelso.

"Can you tell me the best way to go?"

Ian told them how to get there and left them to put it into the van. Meanwhile he telephoned his cousin who was the Police Sergeant in Kelso.

"David, it's Ian. I've just had two chaps in the shop buying a two-seater couch. In fact they are still in the yard putting it in to one of my vans which they have hired. They both look as if they originated somewhere in the Middle East. They have told me that the couch is for Mrs Sutton. I met her once when Hector, her late husband, was a member of the Horticulture club. She's a damned good looking lass but I can't remember her as a person who would buy anything without seeing it and without making a thorough examination."

"Gee! Thanks Ian. That's a mighty useful piece of information. I'm already reacting inwardly as to its true value! I'll have to fly now and perhaps take some action."

"Right, David, they are still in the yard. Good hunting."

David was very keen on gardening. In fact he was well known for all his wins at the annual horticultural competition. This particular year he had done exceptionally well. He was also very astute in solving any problems that occasionally arose in police work. His first reaction now was to rush in to the Inspector's office.

"Colin, I think all is about to begin. My cousin, in Coldstream, reports that two foreign looking guys have just bought a couch, said to have been ordered by Mrs Sutton. It hasn't been ordered, of course, but they are on the way to deliver it at her house. There is not much time left but I have thought of an immediate defence action. You will perhaps remember that I always protect my horticulture pre-competition plants under a large and thick stretch of netting to keep rabbits away?"

Colin said that he remembered.

"It's kept in place by heavy steel pegs. At this time of the year the stretch is neatly folded and stored. You will recall that there is a small balcony above the front door of Mrs Sutton's house. We could have two of our team concealed on the balcony each taking an end of the netting. The netting should have attached to it sufficient steel pegs to give it weight. I envisage that the two transgressors will get as near as possible to the front door. Each of them will be gripping with one hand an end of the couch, the other hand will most likely be in a pocket holding a gun. At an appropriate time our lads will drop the net. They will also be armed.

"Also, in my opinion it will be most likely that Curtis will take up an attacking position at the rear of the house. He will be thinking of breaking in as soon as he hears action taking place at the front door. His action is most likely to involve a metal tool to force open a back door and, then, to enter the house shooting madly at any of its occupants. In connection with my gardening hobby I own an extremely forceful water pump, the jet of which, with or without the assistance of electrical power, will knock a victim for six. I will, if you agree, be situated in a window above the forced door and will immediately put the jet into action. I should be most grateful for your approval."

The Inspector was silent for several seconds. Then he

spoke. "David I have listened very intently to what you have said. The problem, as I see it, is that we have very little time for the action you propose. If you think you can make all the arrangements in the time remaining you have my full support. Your main concern will be to obtain speedily your netting and pump. I am prepared for you to be in control of the operation. I shall however, if there is sufficient cover, conceal myself at the rear of the house, subject, of course, to my exclusion from your water jet! Firstly, though, I shall speak to Derek and remind him that his main concern is the individual protection of Linda Sutton and Stan Watson. While you are gathering your gear I will give instructions to all our staff. Good luck."

David, feeling immensely pleased that his proposals had been accepted, dashed away, after securing one of his staff to assist with the gear collection and warning everyone to stand by, above all other needs, for possible additional instructions. The collection of the garden equipment did not take long and, on return, he gave orders for the actions to be taken, by each and every member of staff. One of the latter was made responsible for bringing first aid equipment and being prepared to give immediate medical assistance, where necessary.

It was hoped that everybody was ready for action. The garden netting, equipped with sufficient weights, was hidden but ready for immediate action. The operators were also hidden. At the back of the house every upstairs window was ready for immediate opening and two of the water jets were just waiting to shoot water at an enormous speed. Inspector

McDougal had managed to find a tree bordering the house that was dense enough to hide his presence.

Then it happened! The van entered the driveway and moved towards the house. It stopped in front of the doorway and its two occupants jumped out. They leaned far into the van and pulled the couch out and placed it on the ground. They lifted it to a position near to the steps in front of the door. One of the men rang the doorbell.

Linda shouted "Coming. I'll not be a moment!"

With the couch gripped firmly at each end, the men still managed to pull a gun quietly out of each pocket. They were primed and ready for the slaughter. But then, like an outbreak of thunder and with great speed, the netting fell to the ground, imprisoning the two men. Both suffered the landing of the heavy steel pegs and struggled to escape from the heavy rope and wire. They no longer possessed their guns as they had been knocked from their grasp; the men had become entangled in the netting, and the more they struggled the more they became entangled. From above they were commanded to put their hands up. This was said with all sincerity but could not be achieved by the restriction of their muscles. It did not take long, however, for handcuffs to be put on and for the normal arrest warning to be given.

Meanwhile, on hearing the bell ring, at the front of the house, Curtis pounced on the door at the back. His large steel chisel was already prising the door open when he was hit by a mighty frightening force. Within seconds he no longer possessed his gun or chisel. The all powerful jet of icy water was completely blinding him and, even with closed eyelids, his eyes were stinging like mad. To his relief, the water eventually lost its intensity and came to a stop. He was handcuffed and the arrest declaration given to him.

Dripping with water as though he were the victim of an atrocious wave from an ugly sea, he raged and raged about the treatment that he had just suffered. Standing before him was Inspector McDougal, to whom he issued the foulest language that any human could suffer. He was marched to the front of the house to stand with the attackers Kahmed and Aliyah. Linda approached him as he rudely swore at her.

"Now," she said, "you are going to suffer some of the agony which you gave me." Then she turned away and retreated back into the house.

Great secrecy had been placed on the police action to disarm and arrest without any physical suffering to them or the detainees. But, as sometimes happens on these occasions, a crowd of curious spectators had already gathered in the driveway to Linda's house. Those arrested were quickly driven away to the cells of the Police station.

"Inspector McDougal, can I have a word before you return to the station. I want to thank you so much for the excellent work that you have all done. There is no doubt about it but you have saved our lives and nobody has been hurt. I would like to say also that we owe so very much, in particular, to Sergeant McMillan. We all hope that he is rewarded in some way. I would like it very much if we could take everyone to the local for a drink."

"Yes. I see no harm in doing so but we'll have to make it pretty short, if you don't mind, in case any of us is wanted."

It did not take long for everyone to be gathered in the pub's private room. Linda, Stan, Derek, the protection man, and to everyone's surprise, David and Anne. David arrived home a few days earlier but because everything had happened at such short notice he was not advised of the impending attack. Inspector Colin McDougal, Sergeant David McMillan, and the two Constables, already known, perhaps for eternity, as the 'netters'. In no time at all, Linda organised everyone's drink, including, to her surprise, a half pint shandy for Derek. She started the drinking session going by giving her thanks and those of Stan for the amazing action that had taken place.

"I would also like to give special thanks to the gardener who had demonstrated to everyone how important it was to have a piece of netting for keeping unwanted guests, especially at Hogmanay, from your home. A jet stream was also very useful for those who never used the front door!"

Her brief words brought great acclaim from everyone else. Fortunately, because of the company no one suggested driving home!

CHAPTER SIXTEEN

Abdullah Mohammed - alias Donald Smith - sat in his office. His thoughts were taken up by the plan to kill Stan Watson and Linda Sutton. Had it, by now, been achieved? It was two days since he had asked Curtis about its achievement. Their removal would put an end to his concern about the possibility of instant recognition by Watson. There was a knock on his door by his Secretary, Kaleem. Hoping that nothing disastrous had occurred, he shouted, "Enter!"

X, whom he had not seen for several months came in. He stood to welcome him.

"Delighted to see you; I have been wondering when I would see you."

"Is there any further news on Curtis? I have been away for the last few days and had assumed that, under his management, no further disasters would occur."

"As far as I know, all has been going well. He told me two days ago that, with the help of Kahmed and Aliyah, there would no longer be a problem."

"Well, I can tell you, Mohammed, there has been. Apparently some ridiculous scheme had been adopted of buying a couch and taking it to the house of Mrs Sutton, where Watson was staying. She, together with Watson, were to be shot as soon as they came to the door. Curtis was to take up his position at the rear of the house and, on hearing the doorbell, he was to break into the house, shooting to kill any of its occupants. All this was bloody useless. Nobody was killed. There was no firing from Curtis and his team and they were all arrested. Curtis, with his past, is likely to get fifteen to twenty years."

For several minutes Mohammed did not issue a word. He was obviously praying. Then, in a quiet voice, which was unusual for him, he said. "I am astonished. I have known Curtis for many years. He has always succeeded on his missions. I had assumed that there would be no difficulties with this one. I can only pray to Muhammad for help."

"Yes, of course. You will realise that we shall have to change our original thoughts. This is a catastrophe for us. We cannot undertake what we had originally planned. We have now lost five operatives, all possessing skills in their various ways. To progress as we wished, we need new recruits who will, of course, need training. We need to rebuild and, for this, we have to rebuild our economy. Our finances are in a bad way, and above all else, we must concentrate on them. Our first job has to be a meeting of our council. What are your thoughts on this?"

"I'm in agreement with everything you have said X. I don't think there will be much difficulty in arranging for our meeting to be held here, in Scotland."

"Yes, I agree, but I'm not terribly sure about your position here. I suspect that the Police forces are being built up here in Edinburgh. We must also remember that three of our operatives are now in police hands in addition to the two who had imprisoned the Sutton woman. The police could be trying to persuade them to be giving helpful information in return for their efforts to obtain a reduction in their sentences. That information could, quite easily, be a reference to your existing office. We have, you will remember, permanent accommodation in Inverness. There, we also have good office accommodation and computer connections. I would suggest that you transfer at once. I would also recommend that you do this today."

"Yes, I agree entirely. I will also take Kaleem with me."

"Good. For the moment I will keep my existing telephone numbers and house accommodation, but unless anything really serious crops up I don't wish to hear from you for the moment. I will advise you later of our new codes. Good luck."

"And to you, X."

CHAPTER SEVENTEEN

David Watson. Stan Watson's cousin, had because of his national position, been chosen to act as Chairman of the Committee elected to review the extent to which Scotland could be vulnerable to atrocities from native or foreign organisations. A Scottish Executive Cabinet's representative was present together with Chief Superintendent Macmillan, acting for the Edinburgh Police forces. The relative Chief Superintendents for other regions of Scotland were also present. Colonel John Frostier was present for the Armed Services.

After welcoming all those present, the Chairman began: "We are all well aware, from the dreadful recent atrocities in London, that a foreign organisation was within the U.K. to destroy the citizens and economies of the United Kingdom. The whole of our country had been alerted by these monstrous activities. Whether or not there are separate organisations acting independently is not known. What we do know, however, is that there are currently signs of a native or foreign body already acting, possibly separately from the murderers in London, to cause as much damage as possible. As far as we believe, they are not a large party but we have already reduced their followers by seven people.

"Some of you may not know how this kicked off. For your benefit, I shall say that it began with the incognito arrival, from Tallinn, of a person who had spuriously obtained, for the purpose of avoiding immigration control, the help of a somewhat naive Brit. That person's name is Stan Watson, who at Tallinn, made his ship's holiday cabin available for the use of the intending illicit immigrant. Meanwhile, Watson proceeded to Dover under normal travel arrangements. On arrival he made his way for payment, as arranged, to the nearest public convenience. Prior to his entrance Watson noticed that he was preceded by another person. He decided to wait until his exit. Before Watson's entrance, however, an unknown person, dived out of the convenience and speedily made his way to escape in his car from Dover. On entering, Watson found his predecessor lying dead on the floor. He had been knifed but no knife was found."

The Chairman continued: "The man, making his hurried exit, overtook a police car whilst still driving in Dover. He continued, outside Dover, to break the speed limit and was eventually stopped by the police car and was taken to the Police station. There, he was arrested under the belief that he was the person responsible for the 'convenience' murder. Erroneously, he was allowed an unknown visitor. Whether he was accepted as a genuine lawyer is not reported, but shortly after his departure the prisoner died from poison.

"Surreptitiously, however, his photograph was taken. Watson immediately recognised the photo as belonging to the person who persuaded him to assist in the

Tallinn episode. Watson has also gallantly helped by a lengthy examination of national photographs of persons previously arrested. He has found that the 'Tallinn' person was known as Abdullah Mohammed or Donald Smith now believed to be residing in Edinburgh. Watson is my cousin and, as a token of my hospitality I asked him to come and stay at my house. On arrival he and a friend, who is also a neighbour, grew very fond of each other and the two of them went for a walk in the Kelso region. Not long after walking he was shot in the shoulder and taken to Edinburgh for hospital treatment. Shortly after this, his friend, Linda Sutton, was captured by John Curtis, a Kelso acquaintance of mine, and imprisoned in a basement flat in Edinburgh. By her sheer intelligence and guts she managed to escape from her two gaolers who were then arrested by the Edinburgh police. She then returned to her home in Kelso and gave refuge to Stan Watson and her protector provided by Edinburgh police. Within a couple of days, three armed people attacked her home.

"Thanks to the excellent foresight of the Kelso police they were captured without any injury. One of the arrested people is Curtis. Without any doubt, the apparent desire to kill Stan Watson is because he is the only person, known by us, capable of recognition. Now, I should welcome hearing your thoughts on the actions we should now take?"

"Do you think that Edinburgh is a possible target for acts of extreme terror?" said Chief Superintendent Mac-Millan of Edinburgh.

"I think that because it is the capital city of Scotland and the fact that it holds many activities attracting enormous groups of people that it is at greater risk. I am thinking here of such events as the Edinburgh Festival. Also, other attractions in cities such as Glasgow, Dundee or Aberdeen cannot be dismissed as unlikely targets. Airports, for instance, cannot be ignored in any part of Scotland. If any threat embraces the possibility of suicidal bombing, then we must take every conceivable precaution."

"From the incidents that have already taken place, in particular, the availability of criminals resident in Scotland, are we, automatically, to accept that Scotland is at great danger?" queried Glasgow's representative.

"In giving consideration to this question we would have to know how long have the 'criminals' been living in Scotland and whether or not they have succeeded in obtaining employment. I would like to know under what circumstances they are already believed to be 'criminals'. In the present climate it might be natural to think of them as 'criminals' but without any evidence it would be wrong to think categorically that they represent a great danger to Scotland. Were these people immediately to take up residency with known criminals we would be very wise and, perhaps justified, in thinking of them as a great danger to Scotland. We have to acknowledge that where people reside for a long time in a particular area, they are likely to have a more learned knowledge of the occupations of others. This may or may not be advantageous to those seeking to benefit from that knowledge."

"In what area do you envisage that military help can be of great help?" asked Colonel Forster.

"I think that most help would be needed where the number of wounded people is so great that there are insufficient ambulances available for a quick transport to a hospital. Military hospitals might also be needed where there are insufficient beds available in certain areas. Help might also be needed where the number of available fire engines is insufficient in a particular area. It is also within the bounds of possibility that naval assistance might be needed where, in remote areas, immigration laws were being broken. H.M. Customs also give a valuable service where there are attempts to smuggle drugs."

After a brief pause, he continued. "I trust that we do not lose sight of the possibility that attempts may be taken to manufacture explosives locally. Acetone peroxide, for instance is easy to make but difficult to detect. This is also known as the 'Mother of Satan', which is highly unstable and liable to explode with the slightest of tremors or with even a rise in temperature. Many attempts to make bombs have resulted in the deaths of handlers in the use of, for example, triacetone triperoxide, occasionally known as TATP. There are many examples of attempts to make explosive material and I am conscious of the fact that I am a complete novice in an area well known to many of you."

"Don't be so modest."

"It might be useful, however, to give an early consideration to any explosive material that could be used by terrorists. For that purpose, without mentioning at this time our interest in such a query, it might be helpful to consult university lecturers about the availability of chemical substances for the manufacture of explosives.

"Well, gentlemen, this has been our first discussion of this nature. I hope that it has been of some help and that we can meet again fairly soon. Finally, it would be a great honour to me if you would all join me for a drink at the nearest local."

It was a terrific summer morning. The sun was shining brilliantly and, where there were gaps in the curtains, the cloudless sky was at its best. Stan could just hear Derek opening the front door. He was always in a hurry at this time of the morning and most days it would be a good half hour before he returned. His whole time was taken up by a most scrupulous examination of the outside of the house, the garden and the surrounds. Funny, really, after the great success of the Kelso Police there had been no relaxation of the care given in his protection and that of Linda. Also it seemed that Derek was going to be around for much longer than he had thought. The risk of attack must be as strong as the police ever thought there would be.

This guy, Curtis - what an odd guy he was. Kelso was such a pleasant place to live in. The country was spectacular. He had a nice house and his wife – if that was what she was – had good looks and was well liked. She had disappeared, of course, since his arrest. Were there any children? If there were, they were kept well out of sight. They could be old enough to be in their twenties.

But what about Curtis? Was he really dependent on foreigners for his livelihood? He must be paid well! The whole thing could not be a gag. Everything began with one illegal immigrant and it was not he.

Linda lifted her head from the pillow and, smiling broadly, said; "Hello my darling. Have you been awake for a while?"

"Oh! Yes, beautiful! I've been lying here thinking 'what a lucky guy I am!' But just when are we getting married?"

"Ah, very soon! Today perhaps!"

"Right we'll go into Edinburgh and get you a wedding outfit. Then a long stay in the most expensive suite available. A balcony too. I say, is it possible to make love on the balcony?"

"Of course but wouldn't it be better in a big, gorgeous bed?"

"Oh yes, yes. With a litre of "Grouse or Highland Park'. A malt, of course!"

"Sorry to spoil the fun but are you still determined not to get married until our friend Mohammed is behind bars?"

"Dear Linda, I'm afraid so. I'm convinced that both of us are still targets and, gruesome as it sounds, neither of us could exist without the other. Remember too, the Police are still providing a protector, so they must still be thinking of the risk."

"Yes, you are right. But, my love, remember that you might not always be right."

"Yes I am! One thing I was curious about, though, is does Curtis have any children?"

"Yes, he has two sons. I've not seen them for years. The younger one was quite nice but I could not stand the elder. He was a nasty piece of work. Spoilt by his father, I believe. Now that Curtis is awaiting trial in Edinburgh the whole family seems to have disappeared."

"Heavens, look at the time. I can hear Derek moving around. He must be making breakfast. I must hurry in case he's alone."

After taking a shower, he was in the kitchen. "It's a nice morning, Derek. How is everything going?"

"Oh fine. I had one or two talks with some of the locals. Everyone seems very friendly and helpful. I've even had an invitation to play rugby in the local team. It's a good few years now since I've played. I suspect that they are desperately short of players but I said that I would lend a hand. I gave a warning that they should not hope for too much!"

"I am not a rugby player myself but I should like to watch."

"They want me to play next Saturday. Do you think Linda would mind if I started practising on the front lawn? I can get a friend to collect my gear and bring it here. I could easily repair any damage to the lawn."

"No, she'll not mind. In fact she'll be delighted to come along. Ah! Here she is now. Linda, Derek has had an invitation to play for the rugby team on Saturday but he badly needs to practise. It's not the Melrose Sevens! At least I don't think so! Would it be okay if he practised on the front lawn?"

"No problem. I should be delighted to see him running around. There's one condition though!"

"What's that, dear?"

"It's quite simple – the condition is that he allows me to run around with him passing the ball at every angle. Perhaps you might feel like cutting down a couple of the eucalyptus trees and the three of us can make a goal. It won't be too high though!"

"Gosh, that's absolutely terrific, Linda. Can we start this today, please?"

"Of course we can. We've got a felling axe for the trunks."

There was now terrific fun and excitement in Linda's house. The two uprights were reasonably straight and, although the cross bar was not actually as straight as it might be, it offered great fun for practice. Derek was able to meet the team and have some practise at the grounds in the evening. The great day arrived. Linda and Derek surreptitiously hid some wine and sandwiches in a carrier bag. They were given a good seat after wishing Derek 'good luck". The Kelso team came out on to the pitch followed by the opposing team. Both teams used the initial time for passing and kicking the ball into their goal.

"Stan, where on earth is Derek?"

All the players of both teams were on the pitch but there was no sign of him. The Captain was looking around the field and the Ref began to look over towards the clubhouse. Stan jumped out of his seat and ran like mad towards the pavilion steps. Suddenly. Derek stumbled out of the doorway. Blood was flowing like mad over his vest and he was desperately clutching his chest. Panting like mad, Stan reached him and, grabbing a towel that had been left on the steps, he rolled it and pressed it gently on the area of the flow.

At the same time he yelled to Linda, "Rush to the Ref for protection and at the same time use your mobile to telephone for immediate medical treatment and then the police. Telephone also for medical help from Anne. Above all else keep very close to the Ref and don't let anyone come near you – particularly anyone wearing a rugby strip. I'll stay with Derek until the ambulance arrives."

Stan addressed the wounded policeman. "Derek, I am going to keep this towel pressed on your chest. I shall keep one of my arms around you. Now lean on me. I shall hold you so that we can both sit on the Pavilion steps. Okay, bend your knees, gently now. I'm with you all the time. Medical help is on the way. Try to relax. I'm here to look after you."

Suddenly, Derek pressed closely to Stan's body. He jerked his head forward. Blood was now gushing from his mouth. He was trying to speak. Stan raised one of his arms across his shoulder and said gently. "Derek hold on. Just a little longer. Medical help is on the way. Linda and I love you."

"I... I'm.... sorry. I tried.   It... Curtis." He fell forward, limp and lifeless. Tears began running down Stan's cheeks. It was now too late.

Two ambulance men, carrying a stretcher, dashed up the steps. They examined Derek but they could already see the situation. One of them turned towards Stan and with his arm across his shoulder, said, "We are very sorry. Can we help? If you are up to it we'll take you along to the hospital."

"That's very kind of you but I must find Linda, my friend. She will be heart broken. Ah! There she is." He put his arms around her shoulders and hugged her as tight as he could.

"Come my darling. Let's get home as fast as we can."

CHAPTER EIGHTEEN

Stan took Linda home as soon as he was able to assist the Police in their initial questions. In the early evening, Inspector McDougal appeared at the door together with a young Police Constable.

"Mrs Sutton, I'm sorry to have to call after this afternoon's dreadful happening. May I introduce you to Police Constable Angela McCallum."

Both women greeted one another.

"She has kindly offered to come along to help pack Derek's clothing and take them away to give to his parents. I wanted to let you know, as soon as possible, that the Chief Constable of Edinburgh has very gallantly procured someone to act immediately as your protector. He is a very nice young chap and will do his utmost to ensure that you and Stan have the best security possible. He will arrive this evening because we are anxious to see that there is no gap in the protection we have to offer. Under the circumstances, I realise that having a newcomer to the house at this time could present further stress to your household. We think, however, that this is the best solution we can offer."

"Inspector, your visit is very welcome. Both Stan and I are terribly upset about what has happened. Derek was such a nice chap and we were very fond of him. The sorrow is enormous but, as it is, Stan and I have both lost close relatives in our families and we have learned to accept such losses. Under the circumstances, too, we accept your wisdom in providing a new protector. I am absolutely certain that Derek was convinced that we were about to be attacked when, acting, as he thought in our defence, he was stabbed. Now, may I offer you coffee or, even something stronger?"

"That's very kind of you. Angela and I would be pleased to have coffee."

"Why not try a dram." interrupted Stan in a whisper. "Linda will be having coffee or tea while she lends a hand to Angela in Derek's room."

'"You're quite a devil, Stan, you know fine that I'll go for the dram. Malt! Please."

"Right. Colin, your command will be obeyed!"

"Well. Stan. This has been a terrible development. We all knew Derek and respected him. At the moment we are at a loss over the question as to who killed him. The attacker escaped by smashing the changing room window. I think we can say, without any doubt, that this was a prelude to knifing you and Linda. I should welcome very much any thoughts you may have."

"I awoke very early in the morning. The sun was shining brilliantly. Linda was sound asleep and I lay there reminiscing. Then my thoughts went to Curtis and I wondered how could he, living in such a wonderful place as Kelso, act as he has done. Was there a family? Were there any children? When Linda was awake, I said that I was curious about the existence of any children. Apparently there were two sons. She had not seen them for years. The younger one was quite nice but she thought the elder was a nasty piece of work. She believed that, when he was a child he was spoilt by his father. The whole family have disappeared since his arrest. Now, I cannot help feeling that he had something to do with Derek's death."

"This is very helpful, Stan, and it's a line of investigation we must take immediately. I'll just wait until Donald Cummings arrives. At no time must there be a gap when you have no protector. You might find it more irksome now but neither of you can open the door to a visitor without Donald's presence. There's your front door bell ringing now. I'll answer it."

Suddenly there was a very loud crash and the front door was smashed open with the help of a small eucalyptus trunk. Colin dived behind the upright of one of the side doors. Already, he had his gun in his hand, ready to shoot. He was able to see that a revolver, held by a young man in the front porch, was pointing up the hall.

"Drop your gun immediately," shouted Inspector McDougal. "If you don't I will right now shoot you to the ground."

"And I'll shoot mine." said the young guy swearing profusely. "Look what you've done to my Dad. Now you'll pay for it. Aye, it's your turn now."

He pulled the trigger of the revolver and the shot went flying along the length of the hall. The sound of it was enough

to waken everyone in the surroundings. Then there was another crash. Someone from the garden had run with full speed
and landed on his back, with his arm encircling his neck.

"Drop it right away or you're dead now," said the new
arrival in a voice that brooked no arguments. With that he
pushed his knee into the gun holder's back and at the same
time jerked his forearm round his neck. The gun dropped to the
ground, and within seconds there were handcuffs around his
wrists held at his back.

Stan rushed along the hall to see the Inspector. "Colin,
are you all right?"

Inspector McDougal got to his feet and with one hand
sweeping above his head said. "Friends, Romans and Coun-
trymen, it is my pleasure to introduce Constable Donald
Cummings to you. I'm delighted to commend him for his skill
in a most remarkable rugby tackle and it hasn't cost us a cent
to see it! Donald, may I introduce you to everyone here. Angela
would you please phone the station for transport to take the guy
lying on the floor to one of our cells."

Linda stepped into the middle of the floor and said. "Hi,
Donald, I'm Linda. May I extend to you a very great welcome
to our home. I hope sincerely that you enjoy your stay with us.
Stan is standing next to me and I extend his welcome to you."

Donald shyly said, "Thank you very much."

Stan walked to the centre of the room and said. "Ladies
and Gentlemen. I know that you have certain regulations but
on one of the tables over there you will be able to see coloured
glasses of orange juice. The next table, which cannot be seen,
has coloured glasses of something different. The contents of
all the glasses are not distinguishable. Please have a drink to

be able to give a welcome to Donald and to give thanks to him for what he has accomplished."

Inspector McDougal, with a broad grin on his face, stepped forward and said, "I just love orange juice!"

Everybody clapped and an enjoyable evening began.

CHAPTER NINETEEN

X was now in Inverness. He made his way to the organisation's quarters.

Kaleem, the Secretary, greeted him joyously and took him to Abdullah's room.

"Greetings," he said to Abdullah. "How are you gettingling on in the new accommodation? Comfortable I hope?"

"It's great, X. The sitting room, bedrooms, and kitchen are all perfect. In fact, all is superior to that of Edinburgh."

"Good! Now about our plans, are we making progress?"

"Yes, X. I'm finding everything is ideal for our plans. I've made a preliminary excursion to the north west of Scotland. The Gairloch to Melvaig and Arisaig area is under survey and it looks promising. It seems to be a very quiet region and, hopefully, it should suit our plans. I've yet to enquire from the locals as to the approach from the sea. The ship's skipper will be looking for a safe anchorage site. The main concern is, of course, the ease by which goods can be got ashore. If we are all right for the winds, rocks and currents, it should not be too bad. The first supply is arriving, via Ireland, in a month.

"Our priority is to have the storage premises and transport vehicles ready for our distribution to the south. I hear that, of the heroin found in Britain, 95% is thought to come from Afghanistan. The majority of poppy growing farmers are in the Kandohar region. Afghanistan is said to be the biggest producer of opium. Britain is now giving millions of pounds to the Government in order to wipe out poppy growing and to replace it with new products that will promote new trade. Immense help is also being given to rebuild roads and provide irrigation systems for farmers as an encouragement for the growing of anything other than poppies. It is thought that to succeed, in this respect, it will take many years to accomplish.

"We have now, of course, to maintain an absolute secrecy about our importations. If we succeed, which I think we shall, we will have a good income for the buying and training of our followers. Given time we shall be in a position to own land and govern an immense country in what is claimed by British people to be the so called, Middle East. Britain will be part of our empire. Praise be to Allah!'

"Yes, Praise be to Allah. You refer to storage premises and transport. Are you aiming for storage in the north here or for a depot further south?"

"The north of Scotland would be ideal for the simple reason that it is sparsely populated and deliveries at night would attract less attention. For further deliveries from premises further south, I favour Glasgow. I aim to make that city simply a distribution centre. Drug selling from thereon will become the sole responsibility of the buyer."

"I agree with this."

'Thank you. But transport continues to be a very difficult problem. We have to find a business that will comply entirely with our wishes. Although the company chosen will have the prerogative to act within their own, normal authority we shall impose a very severe reign over the maintenance and condition of their vehicles. We want to avoid any imperfection that might lead to a road stoppage by the Police or other organisation. Equally, we want to have a situation where absolute loyalty is given by the drivers to their company. Consumption of alcohol during driving will attract the severest of penalties from our own staff. Hamad, whom you will remember arranged for me to take over Watson's sea journey from Tallinn, will have complete control over storage and transit arrangements. He will severely punish anybody who fails to follow our instructions."

"What about sea deliveries from Afghanistan? Are the plans satisfactory and will carriers be landing goods in Ireland?"

"No drugs will be landed in Ireland or in other ports. Transit arrangements will allow for all drugs to be hidden in appropriate ship cavities in or near to engine premises. It is hoped that engine oil and the smell of other products will counteract the possibility of discovery by trained dogs. Drug supplies will be conveyed from the ship by boats designed, in the main, for life saving activities. Such boats will be provided with the appropriate chemical for eliminating drug aromas. Precise landing areas will be notified by code to those responsible for landing. Where necessary, appropriate signals will be advised of the exact positions for landing. Where there are adverse conditions, ships will be notified of those areas where landing is not to be taken."

"Good! I am not sure if you are up to date with local news. The guy, provided by the Police to protect Watson and Mrs Sutton, was knifed and killed by Curtis's son at a rugby match. Because of the crowds waiting to see the match, he was unable to get near enough to kill Watson and Sutton. On the night of the killing, he attacked their house but unfortunately was taken prisoner by the newly appointed Police protector. This results in two Curtises awaiting trial. We remain determined to dispose of Watson and Sutton. I'm leaving now but keep me in touch with developments.

"Allah be with you, X."

CHAPTER TWENTY

A week later Derek's parents asked Stan if he could give a farewell in the church.

Stan was sitting with Linda in the third row of the church. On the Minister's indication, Stan walked to the altar.

He said: "Ladies and Gentlemen. Unfortunately, I had not known Derek for a long time. In fact, his parents are doing me a great honour by allowing me to say something in his memory. It was not for a very long time that he stayed with us, at Linda's house. The Police had asked him to look after us because it was felt that we might be attacked by those with an intent to kill. Derek took the job with great enthusiasm. Nobody could have looked after us better than he. But parallel to this was his marvellous character. He was such a nice person and he looked after us far better than anyone else could. We looked upon him as one of our family. He was asked to play rugby in the local team and his enthusiasm became our enthusiasm. Derek, we are so sad to have to say goodbye to you and, like your parents, Linda and I love you so very much. God bless you."

The next morning, Linda decided that although a change

was as good as a rest a change AND a rest was even better.

"Stan, are you awake? Yes you are! You've just opened your eyes. You're pretending!"

"No, I'm not. I'm sound asleep You're dreaming. If you don't shut up, I'm going to tickle you. Isn't it about time you made some tea? It's your turn. Donald is probably up and patrolling the neighbourhood."

"Look Stan, we've had an awful time recently. I'd like to get away from here and, this time, avoid Edinburgh and go up to Inverness. I've never been further north than Inverness since I was a child. Don't tell anyone but I'd like to be the heroine who found the Loch Ness Monster. I might do it! I'm a good swimmer!"

"Nonsense, the water is as cold as the Arctic and. in any case, you're too young to go searching. There's a hotel on the banks of the Ness. It has a very large window overlooking the water. At window level there are rows and rows of armchairs, all taken by tourists, almost fighting to be the first people to sight the monster racing along the surface of the water. Of course, behind them, is a large bar with a never-ending queue of people ordering their favourite drink. Soon, every piece of floating wood, irrespective of its size, is seen, by those still awake, to be the beast or part of the beast swimming along. Immediately, the bar becomes busier than ever for the purpose of celebrating the first sighting of the 'beastie' of Loch Ness."

"You do talk rubbish," chirped Linda. "One of these days someone is truly going to sight the monster. When that happens, all the inhabitants of Scotland can have a litre of Highland Malt made available from all the casks of whisky currently maturing in every distiller's warehouse. Anyway I'm determined that we go and, at least, have a wee peep looking for the all time survivor."

"Whatever you want!"

"Changing the subject though, even as a child. I enjoyed so much the absolute beauty of the mountains and the lochs. Now, I'll let you into a secret, I have a great friend, Maggie, who has a cottage not far from Gairloch. I've already spoken to her on the phone and she says that she would be delighted to make it available for the next couple of months. She works for the Foreign Office and has just been offered a post at the British Embassy in Warsaw. Now, don't tell me that you have some other appointment because it won't work. I've told her that we are going. She has already got the key in the post. Donald is free and, as a keen angler, is jumping for joy."

"Oh, Linda! You've got me all wrong. Nothing would please me greater than spending some time in the Highlands. I love Scotland, especially the North. There's some good hills and mountains to climb near Gairloch and Donald can, perhaps, keep us supplied with fresh salmon and trout! Let's start packing!"

"Donald tells me that golf is his favourite game. You can both squeeze your clubs into the boot of the car. Can we have a bet on who'll win?"

"Definitely not! He might win!"

The keys arrived the following day.

There were many hotels at Strathpeffer but although they had thought of staying the night at this delightful place, they decided to keep going. The road could be tricky at times. Because of the many turns and variation in the gradients it was hardly a race track. The scarcity of the oncoming traffic, however, was a great asset and they made great progress. But it was the scenery and the variation in that scenery which attracted the most admiration. Loch Maree was on one side and on the other were the most majestic mountains imaginable. Was it possible to climb them? Since, historically, they came from nowhere, not many souls had stood on such a vast area. Soon they were driving into Gairloch.

"Can you see that large building on the left side, overlooking the loch? At one time it was a very expensive hotel. Every year the English Lord Chief Justice stayed there for his holidays, or so I was told. Of course, there were not many people living in this area at that time. I have often wondered, though, if he knew that, not very far away, illicit distillation took place regularly in the nearby hills! Oh Hell, Donald, I've been blethering again" muttered Stan. "But we have overshot Gairloch. Linda's friend Maggie told Linda that it was a mile or so before we got to Gairloch."

"Sorry Donald," exclaimed Linda, "but I've been miles away wondering if goats could wander around on those mountains!"

"That's okay," said Donald, "I've been asking myself if there are many deer running around up there! I can turn back at the opening just ahead."

"That must be it," yelled Linda, "on the right there. It looks very nice."

They were delighted. There was a bedroom, a bathroom, sitting room and a large kitchen downstairs. Upstairs were two bedrooms and a bathroom. Donald was pleased with his bedroom on the ground floor. One of the bedrooms above, with an impressive view of the loch, delighted Linda and Stan. To their surprise, the kitchen table was neatly laid out with food and a note to say that there was a pan on the cooker loaded with soup. They began eating immediately when the phone rang. It was a Mrs Martin welcoming them. She would see them later in the day and that she would come to clean the house three times a week if that were satisfactory to them. How on earth did she know that they had arrived?

"This really is great," said Donald. "I am sorry to say, though, that I have been ordered to be with you every day and night. I hope that you don't find this a little trying but I'll do my best not to be intrusive."

"Oh that's excellent for me," declared Linda. "There has to be a clothes shop nearby and, of course, a chemist shop. I badly need underclothes and cosmetics. Stan refuses to enter such shops with me and I have a feeling that you will be delighted to give me advice."

By this time, Stan was in tears with laughter, whilst Donald's face got redder and redder.

"A bloody good idea!" chuckled Stan. "I can go to a pub whilst Donald is measuring waist sizes and receiving advice on nail varnish."

"You're both under arrest," warned Donald as he retreated to his bedroom.

The next few days provided excellent enjoyment for all. The weather was perfect and they all succeeded in climbing the smaller hills and mountains. One day they arrived at Ullapool, a very popular town further north. It faced the sea and at one time had been an important fishing port. Now it was a popular holiday place where on one side of the road there was an abundance of shops and restaurants which benefited from the sea view.

Donald began to park on the pavement side and on crossing to do so Stan suddenly put his arms around Linda and forced her to lie flat on the back seat. The back of his head and shoulders were now all that could be seen.

"Pretend to be kissing but don't expose your face. Donald, stop at the kerb as intended. The guy walking towards us on the pavement is Hamad who, in the London pub, forced me to go to Tallinn to meet Abdullah who took my 'on board' place to travel to Dover."

"Lock the doors and remain low. I'm going to follow him," uttered Donald. "Hopefully, I can arrest him."

It was a few minutes before he returned. "No luck. He walked very quickly and dived into a parked car and made off. Fortunately, I got his registration number and will phone now to see what identification we can get. I'll also confirm if the local Police should be notified at this stage."

It was not long before Donald got a reply on his mobile. It simply stated that 'control had been placed in the hands of David Watson, who would be contacting them very soon. No action should be taken until further information had been obtained about the relevance of Hamad being in Ullapool. It also said the Mr. Watson would notify if an agent was available in the North-West of Scotland.

They felt damned that their plans for an enjoyable

holiday had, undoubtedly been chucked into the sea by no less than the appearance of the guy who, without any doubt, had a few weeks ago set about poisoning his fellow countryman. Even if he were captured it was unlikely that specific proof would show that it was he who had deprived another of his life.

"I'd love to get hold of the bastard." growled Stan.

"Me too," exclaimed Linda. "But what's he doing up here? It has to be that there is something evil going on. I would guess that he's not the type to go climbing or fishing without the help of others."

"I think we should try to analyse what attractions there would be in any of the remoter parts of Britain. It seems to me that if there are those who would want to act illegally they would choose somewhere out of sight and, if that is the case, the importation of dutiable goods or drugs would be the answer. Choose any isolated gulf, of little size but hidden by rocky cliffs and you have the haven for smuggling drugs, preferably at night, in a size reflecting great wealth. From Gairloch, northwards or even southwards, there are many inlets that could be admirably utilised."

"I agree entirely." said Linda.

"Me too," agreed Stan. "I think we should head back immediately for Gairloch."

They were not far from their quarters when Linda questioned if either of the two others had noticed that a man, occupying Mrs Martin's house, was of a darkish skin that could easily indicate a Middle Eastern upbringing. Whether or not he was a husband or a lodger was not clear.

Both Stan and Donald had to admit that they had not seen the man in question. She assumed that it was just a case of her feminine curiosity. On arrival at Gairloch, Linda gathered together the various parcels of food and jumped out of the car. There were just two letters on the doormat. One was of no importance. The other was a letter from David saying that he had heard of their news and would be making contact soon.

Whilst Stan poured out several drinks, Linda began making what she hoped would be a most tasty dinner. Donald took a shower in his room but he was not long before settling down in the sitting room and downing his drink. There was not anything of excitement on the T.V. and, when Linda shouted that dinner was ready, there was a mad dash for the kitchen.

After dinner they played a game of Solo. To her delight, Linda was the winner and was even more delighted to be the receiver of several pounds. It was not too late before they went to their rooms. It was well after midnight when Linda awoke to find herself in the arms of Stan. She lightly kissed his lips but he did not move. Something was wrong. What was it? There was a smell of smoke. Suddenly there was a most frightening crash. Stan jumped out of the bed and rushed to the window. There was nothing to be seen but smoke was now floating up the stairs. Grabbing one of his golf clubs and one for Linda, he told her to keep closely behind him.

There was a gunshot followed by another. Neither had the same sound. Deciding not to cry out to Donald and with Linda behind him, he reached the turn in the staircase. Downstairs was now thick with smoke. It was not possible to see the floor below.

He whispered to Linda to stay low and, when he shouted to her, to get out of the front door immediately. Bent low, he crept down several more steps. There was no sound from Donald. On reaching the ground floor he tripped on a body and found himself lying across it. He put his hand forward to raise himself from the floor. His hand was covered in blood but, to his surprise, it gripped a revolver and, with his finger on the trigger, he gently raised himself. The front door was open and he quietly looked out on the small garden before him. There appeared to be nobody there so he quickly turned and raced up the lower staircase. Quickly he grabbed Linda and partially carried her down the stairs.

"Make for one of the bushes and throw yourself on the ground behind it," he whispered.

Turning, he made for Donald's room and. by feeling the floor, he found him lying there. "Oh hell," he muttered, "don't be dead."

Gently he lifted him into his arms. There was a quiet, obviously in pain, response. It was Donald whispering.

"I've been hit. See if you can get a type of tourniquet to go around it. You'll see where to put it from where the blood is rushing out. Now, see if you can get us both out of the house. It will probably explode in no time."

Grabbing him gently and lifting him to his feet, Stan managed to get the injured Donald onto the lawn. After crying out instructions to Linda, he rushed back into Donald's room. He knew from past observations that his official mobile would be lying on the bedside table. After grabbing it he dashed from the room, the phone at his ears. He managed to get through to the local Police to tell them that most urgent medical service was needed. And that a person, who appeared to be dead, was lying in the hall of the house. He also told them that a fire engine was needed immediately.

Linda was, already, attending to Donald and with her help, he managed to get him further away from the house. It was just in time, for a large explosion sounded out from the house; it was soon emblazed by massive flames bursting from the windows above.

It was not loo long before the Police arrived supported by an ambulance. The ambulance's paramedical was able to tell them immediately that a helicopter had already left Inverness. Meanwhile, the Police were able to tell them that a fire engine was on its way. They did not think, however, that in the light of the explosion and the resultant fire, that it was likely that anything could be saved. After a thorough examination of Donald in the ambulance, the paramedical insisted on examining both Linda and Stan.

Access to the man shot in the house remained impossible. One or two people, including a very upset Mrs Martin were already standing at the gate to the garden. Stan went over to talk to her. She was now sobbing profusely. Stan put an arm round her shoulder to give her comfort. She cried out, "What will poor Alice think? The house was the adoration of her life."

"Mrs Martin, I have to ask you, I'm afraid, are you alone in your own house?"

"Yes, usually, but a few days ago, a man came to the door to ask if I could possibly give him lodgings for a few days. He's such a nice man and I agreed. He insisted on paying me in advance. The only thing is that he's very particular about what he eats. He never touches pork or beef and will never take a glass of wine."

"Would you mind very much if I asked a Policeman to come over to talk to you?"

"Not at all."

Of the Policemen present there appeared to be an Inspector, so Stan went over to suggest that he had a talk with Mrs Martin. On hearing, also, that he was not very well versed on the fact that Donald had been chosen to give protection to himself and Linda, he suggested that he contacted his cousin, David. This he did, having to shout on the phone to overcome the noise from the Air Ambulance helicopter that was just touching down. David suggested that Linda and he came to his H.Q. to see if further protection could be found.

Although Linda confessed that she was terribly tired, she agreed with Stan that it would be more sensible to accept the invitation. Then she looked sternly at him and said. "Things seem to have gone from bad to worse. Stan, I think, more and more, that we are getting into a situation where the only chance for survival is to fly to some foreign part where we can never be found."

Putting his arm around her, he said. "Oh! I do love you so very much. We are so tremendously lucky in not being shot. Unfortunately we have, for the moment, to stick it out until things get better. Let's get married as soon as we can.

It would be so wonderful to have children. Now, I have to confess, I'm getting more than a little sad because I feel that all the unfortunate happenings are entirely because of me. Added to this is the fact that we do not seem to have any power to prevent what is happening around us."

"I know. First there was Derek and now Donald is in a serious way. Let us pray with all our hearts for a healthy recovery. God be with him, Amen."

"Amen to that," said Stan as he watched the helicopter with Donald's stretcher inside take off.

They walked over to a police car, arm in arm.

Police Inspector Kevin McDougal welcomed them at the Ullapool Police Station.

"I'm sorry that you have had to come so far. I had to come back to my office. I am lost with not being able to keep up with all the information on the dreadful time that you have both been having. Your cousin, who has all the background to the events taking place, has kindly sent me copies of the reports originating in Dover. I cannot understand, though, how it became known that you were staying at a house in an isolated place such as Gairloch. As to the lodger staying at Mrs Martin's home, it is obvious that he was told by someone, who knew where you were staying and gave instructions for your demise. That person was carrying not only a gun but also explosive material. Whether or not he was aware that you were protected by a young but well trained policeman is not known. I would think, however, that he jolly well knew of his existence. The whole episode could rest on a desire for revenge but I don't really think that was the motive for the attack. To my mind, it has to be that you knew too much about their history and, right now, intended to prevent a planned crime from taking place."

"Inspector, both Linda and I share, wholeheartedly, your thoughts. We would add, however, that in the light of the position that you now find yourself in that you are hesitating in accepting that there is but one aim and that is to introduce the immediate smuggling and distribution of drugs. We are dealing here, in our view, with a foreign organisation that most likely needs an income for setting up and training terrorists whose eventual accomplishment is to take over the United Kingdom."

"Yes, I'm with you the whole of the way. Here, however, we are in the hands of others and we have to convince these people, such as your cousin's organisation, the Police, Customs and, if necessary, the Armed Forces. I will write to my Chief Constable in this vein. I hope we can succeed before its too late. I've already brought him up to date, particularly as to your obtaining hotel accommodation here. We can then provide an armed protector."

"Right, that will be fine for the moment. We would not wish to stay here too long because we still fear that there remains much to be found at Kelso. There is also Linda's house to be looked after."

"You have my deepest sympathy. For the moment it seems likely that the murderous organisation which seeks to harm you is temporarily resident here in the north primarily to make money. That being so, it has to be by the illicit importation of drugs. You are still here, though, as a prime target for attacking. That being so I am pleased to provide Constable Mark Munro as your protector. He is a very reliable person, with a good reputation, and I have no doubt that he will, in his career, have plenty of promotions. He will stay, for your protection, in one of the hotel's adjoining rooms. He is standing outside my room and I'll introduce him to you now." He opened the door. "Constable Munro, come in now to meet Mr Stan Watson and Mrs Linda..."

"Sir, Ma'am. How do you do? I'm very pleased and honoured to be asked to look after you. I'm completely at your service."

"Hello, Mark," said Linda, "I too am delighted that I shall be given the opportunity to get to know you."

"Me too." said Stan.

Turning towards Inspector Munro Mark said, "With your permission Sir, I'll take our guests over to the hotel."

The hotel rooms were not luxurious but Linda accepted that it was bearable for a stay that was not too long. Mark's room was adjacent. He examined the locks and decided that they were acceptable. Stan reckoned, however, that a strong kick would allow an easy access. Mark assured them, however, that a Policeman would be on a twenty-four hour corridor patrol even when they were not in the hotel.

"Stan, I think it would be easier to telephone on my mobile rather than use the hotel's phone. I must speak to Alice immediately but she must be in Warsaw by now. I'll try her sister first."

Linda got through after three rings. "Hello, Audrey? This is Linda speaking. I'm afraid that I have very bad news to tell you. I'm afraid that your sister's house in Gairloch has been attacked by a criminal. An explosive material was used causing the house to be destroyed by fire."

"Oh my God! The house was her pride and joy. What can we do? She's already left for Warsaw. I've had no message as yet from her. Give me your address and telephone number and I'll contact you as soon as I can. She has the house insured but I've no idea of the insurer."

"Many thanks Audrey. I'll keep you in touch. Bye."

"Stan, I must, somehow, find out who is the insurer. We'll have to search in Ullapool. There must be somebody who can help. Before we go there I think we must give a lot of thought to what has happened. This character, Hamad. He must have recognised you in Ullapool and perhaps me too. Without hesitation, he was able to have a man equipped with explosive material staying at Mrs Martin's. Was she part of the plot to kill us or was she completely innocent? Does she normally provide accommodation to strangers especially when they appear to be of foreign origin?"

"Well done my dear! I've been having thoughts on the same lines as you but there is also something else troubling me. We have thought all along that a smuggling operation was being planned – but perhaps it wasn't. Why come so far north to import drugs when there are places in the south of England to operate just as well? We know already that, because of us, their organisation has lost at least seven members. Perhaps they have concluded that it is more practical for them to have a northern route for the entry of illegal immigrants. We have assumed, perhaps incorrectly, that they are motivated by a desire to build up their monetary reserves through the sale of illegal drugs. Like hell! They want to have an army of immigrants training as soldiers on some remote mountain in the north here. If we saw a gang of twelve guys running around the crest of mount so and so, we'd think they were undoubtedly the county's running team. In fact we might not give much attention to a rifle firing range. Should our curiosity arouse us, how many of us would want to climb up to such a height or, prior to climbing, walk through swampy heather to get to the foot of a cliff face before searching for the best route upwards? All this on some landlord's estate without a sight of a crofter's cottage?"

"Gosh, Stan, you sound pretty fed up! Let's take my catapult for protection and go north to look for foreign bodies running around half naked."

"No! We can go into the High Street for that, but beforehand, let's go and rouse Mark, our protagonist! We can have a dram and get him a ginger ale or something of an effervescent nature. Best to be alive, I suppose, but I'm getting really fed up. It's entirely your fault, Linda!"

"I know – but it's your round."

Suddenly there was a knock on the door and, in response to hearing Mark's voice, Stan undid the locks. "Are you ready for a drink Mark?"

"Ah, thanks Stan. I'll have a large dram of Highland Park, please!"

Linda could hardly refrain from laughing as they descended the stairs to the bar!

After the drinks they found a Solicitor's office, the clerk of which was able to put them through to an insurer's office which acknowledged that they were the insurers for Alice's house. They would examine the property and advise Alice accordingly as soon as they could obtain the Polish telephone number.

A short visit to the Police Station confirmed that there were no subsequent developments. On leaving the station they discovered that it was possible to take a short trip around Loch Broom. The pilot told them that at one time there were many boats that brought their fishing loads into the harbour but this did not happen much these days. Sometimes their catch would be transferred to a larger vessel for sailing back to its country of origin. They could not help noticing that the further they went the more frequently appeared the number of secluded inlets. With most of them, however, it looked as though it would be impossible, without adequate roping, to climb upwards towards a place that would allow internal access. A return to the sea without a pilot, however, did not look too difficult.

On their return to dry land, Mark, not surprising them as previously, insisted that it was now his turn to buy a round of Highland Park,

"You wouldn't be from Kirkwall, would you Donald?" said Stan.

"Aye, I would! Born and bred. I can't exist without my Highland Park!"

They sat down at the table they had occupied previously and a beer was ordered to accompany the dram. Donald was soon delighted to talk of the Orkneys, and of the tales, told by his father when he spent his holidays, of certain places in the Scottish Highlands. On one occasion, many years ago, in an extremely isolated part of the hills, he came across a guy frequently examining profoundly the territory of the neighbouring hills. It turned out that the person had been born and bred in Cornwall and during his youth he had sailed through the Strait of Magellan to achieve a passage from the Atlantic to the Pacific. He had a marvellous vocabulary of blaspheme uttered in the finest Cornish tongue. He admitted that his job was to discover those who illicitly distilled spirit for consumption. This was usually produced at night time and he showed to my father the remnant of a chaise longue which, placed below ground level, enabled a distiller to produce unseen during the night.

"I think we should be going back." said Linda.

CHAPTER TWENTY ONE

They returned to their hotel. Mark hurried to the bar and very kindly ensured that they all got a double dram of Highland Park. After retreating to their rooms, Stan was surprised to find a note on the floor telling him to go alone to room 131 to learn how to play golf. He knew immediately that it was David who was now in room 131 and that he was to go alone to this room. He realised also that he had to give some explanation to Linda because if he didn't she would insist on coming with him and that would mean bringing Mark along. Linda agreed immediately providing that he did not stay away too long.

After tapping the door lightly he was pleased to see David who gripped his hands with great enthusiasm.

"Stan, it is terrific to see you looking so well. Please forgive me for not phoning you during the last week or so. As you know, I've been made boss man in the hunt for the terrorists and this has meant a lot of meetings with so many different people. I was sorry to hear of the despicable attack on Alice's house. It has taught the people of the North of Scotland to be on their guard against these vile people. Your courageous action in rescuing Donald and Linda was out of this world. The wounding of Donald has been kept as quiet as possible but I believe that there are now signs, early though they may be, that he is recovering."

Stan said that he was glad to hear such news.

David continued: "Quite naturally, I would think, you have been wondering if we actually had an agent in this part of Scotland. Disclosure of this or even entering into discussion on it is very strictly forbidden. The police are unaware but as you are my cousin and have been involved in all the events which have taken place, I think it is only right that you should know. Nobody else, including Linda, can be told. Whether the agent is a man or woman I cannot say but the person concerned has operated commendably over the last few weeks."

"I understand. Loose tongues and all that?"

"Indeed. The most recent gen we have is that at least ten people have landed in the north here without importing illicit drugs. They have all received an initial form of training in terrorism and are now receiving further instructions on physical fitness and on the use of modern weapons. There exists, further north from here, a house hardly known even to the people living in the locality.

"The building is situated in a mountainous area full of wildlife. It provides adequate accommodation for the people undergoing training. Of course, there is deer stalking, fishing and bird shooting in the permitted seasons but all these events are needed to provide a steady income for the upkeep of the house further inland. This house is quite aged but its owner has seen that people staying there are charged a large sum for their keep.

" Invariably, there are no people slaying as guests when

the terrorists are undergoing training further down the glen."

Stan was shocked by the news that the terrorists had permeated so far into Scotland. "Nevertheless, it is great to see you, Dave. You may be looking fine but I can see through your disguise right away! I hope that when all this is over you can persuade that ghastly beard to disappear! But let me ask about Anne. Is she keeping well? And the children, too?"

"Yeah, she's great. The children too. You know, you don't alter, Stan! You're just bloody jealous about my beard! The family, at least, keep saying what a damned good looking guy their father is! Being serious, though, I have to confess that I have not been wearing it in Kelso. I'm pretty sure that there is still somebody there who knows about my whereabouts and yours too, Stan."

"Your serious thoughts are not very far from mine Dave. I'm not really a betting man but I've always thought that there is something strange about Julius. Why, for instance, did he and Curtis always appear to be at loggerheads? If anything, their arguments always appeared more than a little contrived."

"Yes, I agree entirely. Perhaps one of these days the answer will come to the fore. For the moment, though, I think we have to line up our plans for the future. The thoughts of my committee are that we must, as soon as possible, assemble a squad for arresting all the insurgents of the north. For this purpose, Colonel Forster has undertaken to provide a squad of soldiers to overpower those in the north who are under military training for doing goodness knows what. There will also be a detachment of police to deal with arrested persons. As controller, I have decided to be present. Communications will be by mobile phone and I am arranging for a doctor and a mobile ambulance team to be on call together with a helicopter. If you wish I should be delighted to have you with me."

"I should be honoured to be present. My main thoughts, however, are for the safety of Linda. She is a most determined person. I am certain that if she learns anything about the arrangements she will do anything to be alongside me. I cannot help feeling that without me she would be a greater problem than if she were standing next to me."

"Stan, forgive me for mentioning it but I have known Linda since she was virtually a child. She may not have mentioned it to you but in the past she has worked alongside me in the same job. The tasks involved were sometimes in quite dangerous situations overseas. I should be pleased to see you, Linda, and your security guard Mark, standing together. In fact, I have already made arrangements for flak jackets to be delivered to the three of you. As soon as I am able I shall let you know of the time and place."

"Dave, I am most grateful for the help you continue to give me. I hope that I can be of service to you."

"Yes, you can be, by letting me beat you at golf! Cheers for now."

CHAPTER TWENTY TWO

It was seven o'clock in the evening when the order came to assemble at four on the following morning.

"Separate instructions will be issued to each unit. Transport for hotel lodgers will be provided at the door to the hotel. Flak jackets, waterproof clothing and boots are to be worn. Water and sandwiches will be provided. Each unit will be led by army or police personnel. Specific verbal instructions, outlining separate routes from the original vehicle and discharge points will be given in transit.

"Detachment 1, led by Colonel John Forster, will be responsible for the attack on the first building visible from the lane. The building accommodates terrorists. Chief Superintendent Colin McDougal will be in charge of Detachment 2. He will seek to occupy the landlord's house situated about a mile further along the transport track.

"Detachment 2 will proceed thirty minutes ahead of that of Colonel Forster. Telephone cables to either building will be immediate targets for destruction. The attacks on the two targets, including outbuildings, will take place at the same time. The two units will confirm to each other that action has begun. David Watson, who commands the venture, will maintain contact from headquarters throughout the opera-

on. Medical aid will operate from that command. A heli-
opter will also be stationed there for immediate first aid
nd, where necessary, for providing military assistance."

All units left at the allotted time. It was a dark night,
causing more of a hindrance than a help as they entered the
mountainous area. Fortunately there was no rain or mist
but the respective vehicle drivers suffered an enormous
strain in avoiding the ditches which bordered either side of
the track. Eventually, the discharge point was reached and
the last vehicle to arrive was not too late. An appropriate
area for the helicopter to land was quickly established.

A brief conversation was held between David
Watson and the respective commanders. Chief Superintendent McDougal, guided by his illuminated compass, set
out together with his unit. On approaching the first building
which could be barely seen, he ordered a wide detour. Very
few lights were visible. The deviation, in itself, caused
irritating stumbling and sliding but he was pleased that the
occasional cursing was scarcely heard.

McDougal began to worry. There was, as yet. no sign
or distant light of the house. They had been walking for
twenty-five minutes but then he remembered that Colonel
Forster would not depart until thirty minutes had elapsed.
Admittedly, they must have left a useable track until they
made a detour of the first building. Time-wise that would
assist the second unit but even allowing for this, their early
departure would stand them in good stead. They must now
be reasonably near to the house and, so far, no stumbling
accident had justified a delay. Then his second in com-

mand touched him lightly on the shoulder and whispered. "Can you see that faint light on the left there?"

"Ah, that's great, I can. Just as you say! We'll go a few hundred yards ahead and then stop within shooting distance. I want to have two armed people standing at every corner to the house. We can then proceed to every front and back door and on my signal charge into the house. For the moment, though, I have to wait until I hear from John Forster."

"Sir. If it's okay I will circulate to ask if everyone is feeling fit. We should have heard from the other lads before I get back."

By the time that his deputy returned to say that all was well, no message had been received from Colonel Forster.

"Nothing as yet, Ken. I feel that everything is okay but we should be hearing soon."

"'I hope so! I have the feeling, a correct one. I hope, that once they charge they will soon scare the daylights out of them!"

"We live in the age of mobile phones but I think that now is the time to see if there are any ground cables for a telephone. If there are, I think it would be a good time to cut them off. Organise someone to look, please Ken."

"Right away. It will be getting light soon. We really must be at all the doors soon."

A mobile phone chirped into life. "That's my mobile. This must be it. McDougal speaking. Hello, John, all going well? Ah! Great. Okay, 6.45 and we'll be at the front door. Good luck. Bye."

"As arranged, Inspector James, you'll remain here with

twenty men and if my whistle goes you will proceed to the house with guns ready. Two armed men at every corner of the house please, and at the door to every outbuilding. Telephone David Watson and John Forster to say we have started."

Led by Chief Superintendent McDougal, the police detachment ran across the yard to the main door of the house. Separate units ran to the back to cover doors and windows. They got to the door when several shots came from the upper windows. The Chief gave the order to break down the door and cover every inside door. Led by himself, he gave the order to proceed upstairs, with every man pausing to allow the man in front the time to take shelter. Then, each man would go forward as soon as the man in front occupied the next refuge. The door to one room upstairs was ajar. The Chief fired his gun into the gap and quickly withdrew for safety to the adjoining wall. There was a loud scream from the room and the sound of a man falling to the floor.

An accompanying Constable dashed inside and shouted "Room safe!" He kicked a loaded gun to the side of the room and pulled a sheet from the bed. He and the Chief then tore a strip of linen from it and bound the leg of the wounded man to control the flow of his blood. He was a middle-aged man of obvious Middle East origin. The Chief left the room giving the Constable an order to remain with the man.

The firing continued from the upper rooms but finally it ceased. Two constables were wounded but, fortunately, not seriously. One house occupant was killed and three were wounded. All were of a foreign origin.

Colonel Forster had a difficult time. As soon as he heard from Chief Superintendent McDougal that his action had begun he ordered an attack. He had taken great care in the positioning of his soldiers, but once they were near to the building a counter attack began. Several of his soldiers were wounded at the outset and he ordered a retreat. A quick call to David Watson was more than helpful.

On hearing of the difficulty facing John Forster, David made instant arrangements for the helicopters to fly to the barracks. With machine guns and hand grenades available, instant havoc was caused to the building from above. This, together with the army's attack at ground level brought an instant surrender. The trainee soldiers who survived came out of the building with their arms held high. Four terrorists were shot dead and there were six badly wounded.

One British soldier was shot dead and, of the others, three were wounded. David allowed Stan. Linda, Mark and Margaret, a medic, to take a truck from the base to journey to the battle area. Mark drove at full speed but on going round a tricky bend in the road he caused the truck to skid into a roadside ditch. None of them was hurt but they found that, without some form of mechanical assistance, they could not get the truck back on the road. They decided to walk to one of the buildings because they knew that some of the wounded were still needing assistance. They proceeded round an isolated bend when suddenly two men jumped out of the track's neighbouring ditch.

"Got you at last." yelled one of them pointing a pistol at them. "Allah is good! I prayed that I would get my old friend Stanley together with his woman Linda. It was only a matter of time."

"And you, Hamad, You'll never escape. Great Britain's Police are waiting everywhere for you. This will be your end."

CHAPTER TWENTY THREE

Hamad kept his gun pointing at his prisoners but he had made a common mistake by being too close to those he had captured. His closeness to his prisoners offered a greater chance of success if one of them, in an attack, leapt forward. His companion was already cutting lengths of rope for tying the prisoners. Mark glared at Stan in a way that could only be interpreted as saying 'be prepared for urgent action'. Linda, in her turn, read the look as meaning 'do something right now'.

Meanwhile, Hamad's soldier continued, in a most laborious way, to cut each piece of rope into a measured length. Linda reacted first. Deviously, but with great speed to attract attention, she put one of her hands on her chest and viciously kicked the soldier in the crutch. Miraculously, Margaret, the medic, with competitive haste, seized a large stone at her foot and crashed it down on his head. With a humour matching Linda's, she cried. "He'll do no more rope cutting today."

Stan, with equal speed and at the same time, dived headfirst towards Hamad and with both hands, forced the arm holding the gun to move upwards with the consequence that the gun fired above the four of them. This and the respective action of the others gave Mark sufficient time to seize his gun from his pocket and fire it into the legs of the insurgent. He fell to the ground screaming with pain. Margaret, coming to the rescue, cut his trousers below his knees so that she would be able to give a thorough examination of the wounds. Fortunately, the bullets not lodging in his bones, had passed through both legs which enabled a prompt application of bandages and the stemming of the flow of blood. Meanwhile, Linda utilised the cut pieces of rope to tie the wrists of the prisoners. The soldier was completely unconscious and, praying that she had not done any permanent damage, she bandaged his head.

Stan jumped very high, saying with great joy. "At long last we've got him. He's tried so hard to murder Linda and I. All of you have acted so brilliantly. If you hadn't we'd not be here. Our everlasting love and thanks to you all for evermore."

It was not long before one of Chief Superintendent's vehicles appeared along the track. It was equipped with wired coil and, once it was attached to their truck lying in the ditch, the vehicle was able to pull it back on to the road. The captives were lifted on to the Police vehicle and taken back to David Watson's base. Stan wanted to search the house further along the valley. Margaret, the medic, wired her headquarters, which gave her permission to go ahead.

"I'm really interested in giving this mansion house a

thorough search. If it were the headquarters for training recruits there must surely be guns and ammunition stored away in one of the rooms."

"Yes," said Mark "and I'll bet it's all tucked away in some hidden place. Most likely it was weapons rather than drugs which were smuggled into the country. It should be fun looking for them."

"I hope there are rewards for finding them," laughed Margaret.

"Of course," cried Linda, "for ladies only. I'm keen to see what they have for covering all their expenditures too. Do you remember all those films of big mansions with wooden panels covering the walls in the rooms? Sometimes, if you were patient, there were secret rooms or, at least, a few safes loaded with cash to be found hidden behind the panels."

"Also the rooms were very often used for concealing forbidden priests!"

"Hey! Wait a moment Margaret, they could be hiding more of their trainee soldiers. Perhaps in secret rooms. We'll all be prisoners again. We'll need to have Mark standing by with his gun pointing at every wooden panel."

"Nothing doing!" shouted Mark. "If I've learnt anything today it's when loaded don't stand too close to your victims."

With a twinkle in her eyes and an enormous grin, Linda muttered. "I wonder who could have said that?"

"It wasn't me!" chirped Stan, "I was never in the army!"

"It's a bit of a mystery to me," said Mark, "as to who actually trained you. Where did you get so much information about the existence of this motley crowd? Where, for that matter, did they get all their information from? Somewhere along the track there must be a Brit involved and why is it so important for that person to succeed. Admittedly, for most big States in history they did not last forever, although for some, such as the Egyptians or the Romans, they made a jolly good show at it. Britain by their power at sea and by establishing an horrific slave trade were as bad as any, but Germany – or perhaps more realistically the evil that existed there at that time – after three attempts in Europe, succeeded finally by racial or national means in an unbelievable destruction of other human beings. I believe, quite strongly, that in the end it was God who ordained that the annihilation of one set of human beings by another could not continue. Thus it was so but are we really able to accept a theological view that the souls of the wicked are destroyed at death?"

"I am sorry, Mark," said Stan, "but I find it difficult to accept an assertion that Britain alone was responsible for the slave trade. It so happened that at that time Britain overtook Spain in its mastery of international sea trade. The demand for free labour came as a result of the existence of warmer climates in lands that were able to produce agricultural products both for consumption and use in a Europe that was only too ready to purchase. Germany managed to obtain part of Africa but, generally, was too late in the race to possess overseas land. Spain, Portugal, Great Britain, France and even Belgium, in its possession of part of the Congo, got there first. It was not until the nineteenth century that Prussia became the leading State of a Germanic confederation. Much credit for this can be attributed to Bismarck's leadership of Prussia in defeating Austria in 1866 and France in 1871. As regards religion I have to confess that I read so little of the Bible when I was given the time to do so."

"Look gentlemen," intervened Linda in what appeared to be a desire to end the dialogue which had arisen between Mark and Stan, "There's the mansion house of who knows who or what! We discussed earlier our plans for searching the house. As far as I'm concerned, and I think Margaret also, it would be better as a start to stick together."

"Okay. We'll stick together," said Stan. "All those in favour, raise their hands politely."

"I'll have my gun ready." whispered Mark.

One of Chief Superintendent McDougal's policemen, a Sergeant, was standing at the door. He and three of his colleagues had been ordered to stay behind at the Mansion House for a few days. One of them was already organising dinner for the evening. He invited them to partake of the meal. They gladly accepted.

There were ample bedrooms and the kitchen pantries were loaded with food. Margaret was particularly interested in searching the library. Whether or not she was interested in looking for particular books was not mentioned but she did not appear to be in a hurry to leave the room. The floor was of light oak blocks and interspersed were colourful rugs of Asian origin. Every wall was adorned by shelves of dark oak and some of the books, backed by thick leather of a significant age, were grouped together. Some of them were the Koran, the sacred text of Islam.

A large fireplace of local stone occupied one of the dark oak walls. The ash in the grate was of wood although to the right handed side of the stone was a large trough of neatly cut peat. Presumably this was dug on the house's estate and when dried brought into the house. No tongs were available for lifting the peat into the fireplace. Margaret did not speak. She sat on a comfortable armchair and continued to stare at the wall containing the fire. Why was the peat container to the right of the fireplace? Her grandmother had always insisted that the peat box be to the left. Her companions, out of courtesy, did not speak, although, if individually investigated, their minds might have revealed a mutual bother as to what was troubling her.

Margaret's gaze had by now dropped to the floor, which she was examining closely.

What was now of concern? thought Stan.

Admittedly, the wood blocks on the left did not shine like those of the rest of the room. Something of a persistent nature was disrupting the otherwise agreeable shine of the rest of the room. Suddenly, Margaret's eyes brightened. She walked across the room and knelt at the spot where she had previously gazed. With a handkerchief she rubbed the floor and then raised her eyes above it to the wooden panel adjoining the stone support of the fireplace. Each of the neighbouring panels was then gently pressed, A few minutes passed before anything happened. When it did there wasn't the slightest expression of surprise on Margaret's face. She said nothing as the central panel began to move inwards to reveal downward steps.

Very quietly, Stan walked over the place of egress and

whispered, "We must only talk in whispers and when we go down the steps keep very close together. Mark, if you agree, would you lead with your gun ready, please?"

"Yes, no problem but just in case, I'll leave a note saying 'down the passageway, immediately on your left' and leave it under the vase on the mantle piece. Stan and I have torches and, as I understand it, both Linda and Margaret have them too." The two lasses acknowledged this by nodding their heads.

There were two passageways at the bottom of the steps. One turned to the left and the other to the right. Mark put his finger to his lips and led the way to the right.

Everything was quiet for a while and then they heard voices. Again, Margaret astonished them immensely by whispering to them that there were about four people having a meal, and talking in what appeared to be pash-lo, one of the two official languages of Afghanistan. She admitted that she was not very good at translating their tongue into English but from what she heard she understood that they had lost all their leaders and had come into the secret area merely to escape being captured. It was apparent that, as far as they knew, nobody else was hiding in this or another part of the house. Whether or not there was a door leading from the corridor, where they stood, had to be determined.

"Stan, could you please creep further along this passage to see if there were any doors opening into this room or any other. There is, of course, the route farther back to the corridor on the left but that must lead to a different part of the house. Please advise us if you can't discover a door. We can then follow to see if there is an 'unobvious' entrance, waiting to be discovered in the dark, by any one of the four of us."

Stan nodded and proceeded to creep along the passage. Although he had the greatest faith in Mark, he hoped that nothing dangerous happened to Linda or Margaret. It now seemed rather strange that Margaret, who had appeared as a medic on the scene, was a remarkably well informed person ready, at any stage of their exploration, to become leader. Dave, his cousin, had, with an air of extreme covertness, referred to the employment of a secret agent who had miraculously learned of the surreptitious activities of foreigners in the North of Scotland. Was she that person? If she were, he knew that he must not refer to her very existence. Strange though!

He continued his examination of the walls in the passageway. There was indeed a door on the right hand side. He glued his ear to the door and then gently opened it. With a crash someone pulled it from the other side. Instinctively he put up his hand to protect his head. This was of no avail because it simply was not needed. Two strong men pounded him with blows and dragged him along a corridor. In a spacious, well furnished room he was pushed and tied into a carver chair. The two men left the room and there was not a sound before the door opened. A middle-aged man walked across the room and sat down at the comfortable chair in front of the impressive looking oak desk in the middle of the room.

'"Well, Mr Watson. I'm delighted to meet you. I've been waiting a long time for this honour but now here you are! Excellent! Your gang has been making a dreadful mess of my house and, indeed, of my staff. May I offer you a cup of tea or coffee? You are very quiet; never mind, I could do with a coffee and my servant will bring one for you. You have been making use of an enormous squad of men and it is a form of cheating because I am not actually quite ready for them.

"Ah! Here is your coffee, I shall leave you to take sugar and put in your own milk. How you do it is not my concern. Now let me see. Several of my men have been killed and taken prisoner. You and others have to be punished for this. Tell me though, are you here alone or have you been accompanied by the soldiers or the police? How did you discover an entrance to these, my strictly private quarters?"

Stan stayed mum.

"You're not saying anything Mr Watson. This cannot be so. Now I must change the situation. Sayad, who caught you entering my private quarters, will only be too pleased to obtain information from you about who else could be here and how you and others entered my private house. Of course, you can avoid his methods for discovering the truth by telling the truth. Now perhaps is the time to tell you that Sayad began his working life by learning how to operate the dentist's drill used by his father, a dentist. For various reasons he did not become a dentist – but nothing enjoys him more than discovering how many teeth he has to extract before hearing the truth. Sayad, your services, please."

Stan knew that his time was now very short. Whatever he was able to do had to be done exceedingly quickly. He was now alone in the room. His arms were tied to the arms of the chair. His legs were free. He had one chance only and that was, somehow, to wound Sayad, even if it only affected him for a very short time.

Sayad entered the room. He walked over to an electric wall socket and plugged in a dentist's drill. With a disgusting smirk on his face he walked back to Stan's chair and switched on the drill. He leant over the chair and with his left hand, bent back the face of his victim. He held the revolving drill within an inch of Stan's lips.

"Tell me!" he shouted.

Having quickly said his prayers and summoned all his strength, Stan, with as much speed as he could muster, thrust his right knee into Sayad's crutch. This was quickly followed by a kick from his left leg, which, with equal or perhaps greater force, hit his genitals. Then standing upright he swung his chair, with immense speed, into Sayad's upper body. Quickly he struggled over to the owner's desk and, with his remaining strength, smashed it down on the table. To his surprise it broke, giving him sufficient room to release his arms and with the heaviest piece available he gave a most aggressive overhead stroke to Sayad's head. Retaining the weapon supplied by the chair he ran out of the room and dashed along the corridor thanking God for his help and praying that he would find his friends.

Mark was waiting in the corridor without his torch. He could hear Stan dashing along the corridor. Grasping one of his arms, he whispered, "It's okay, old fellow. Linda is waiting at the door. Everything is under command. Just hang on to my hand and you'll soon be in her arms."

They raced like mad down the tunnel and finally they could see Linda standing in the dim light. She hugged him as hard as she could and pulled him into the library. Mark closed the library panel as soon as he could and stood aside to let Linda and Stan kiss and continue the hugging. He had, in his career in the Police force, seen many horrific injuries but he had never come across a sight of so much blood before. His own arm and jacket and now, Linda's clothing were covered in blood, yet he could see no wound on his friend's body.

"Come to the kitchen Stan. I have a dram and some food waiting for you and then I'm sure that you'll welcome a nice hot shower. We don't know very much about what you have undergone. We completely missed a doorway but we did find an alcove where we hid when three men ran passed us. We were frightened stiff about your disappearance and did not want to be put in a position where we could not be helpful to you. When you left us Margaret raced away to telephone your cousin. A helicopter is on the way with some army lads. With our Police guys we are hoping to be able to completely surround the house. My main fear is that we might not know of an underground passage that exits well away from the house. Anyway let's go for that dram in the kitchen and you could perhaps let me know about the rough time you appear to have had."

"Your very best health Mark," toasted Stan. "Linda and Margaret are going to join us in a few minutes. I shouldn't make fun about it but I do hope that the guys below do not suddenly come flying into the room from the floor below."

"Good Lord, that's all we'd need! Tell me about what happened."

"To be honest Mark, it was one hell of a horror to experience. The owner of the house has, surprisingly a very wealthy looking premises below. He wanted details about the take over of his premises and, to ensure that he was given information he wanted his gladiator to play his favourite game of shoving a dentist's drill into his victim's mouth to see how many teeth he could get before there was a capitulation."

He took a sip of whisky, welcoming its restorative warmth, and continued: "I had one chance and I was praying like mad for help. Fortunately, my legs were not tied to the chair and somehow I managed with all my strength to push my knee into his genitals and with my other leg kick him in that area too! Then, I managed to bang his chest with the chair. The owner's desk was very helpful, because having struggled to reach it, I was able to shatter the chair and use part of it as a weapon to knock Sayad on to the floor. Thank God you were waiting for me in the corridor. I really was at the end of my tether."

Linda and Margaret raced into the room. It was Margaret, this time, who gave Stan an out-of-this world hug.

"Gosh, Stan, we've been so worried about you. I thought that there was something really wrong this time, so I dashed back along the corridor and telephoned your cousin. He promised to get a relief squad immediately and you'll be pleased to know that it has just arrived. Thank God that you are back unharmed. I've already had a word with the guy in charge. He's agreed that we should be allowed to go back into the cellars but only when he gives the word. I hope that's all right with you?"

"No problem. As a matter of fact I want to go back to have a look for something secret in the owner's desk. I'm hoping to find something of value, perhaps even in a secret drawer."

"Me too! It's my turn," said Linda laughing, "to discover something valuable!"

CHAPTER TWENTY FOUR

The invasion of the quarters below the ground floor began. Although there were one or two people badly wounded, everybody was pleased that nobody had been killed. Stan was very upset to hear that one of the badly wounded was Sayad but, as he was told by the original team that ventured into the cellars, there was no alternative to the action that they had been forced to take. It was known by those who had worked in the house that captives had actually been tortured to death by Sayad.

Stan led the way into the entrance from the library. They were soon in the passageway and to their surprise they discovered that there were lighting facilities on all the walls. Because of this, they were soon entering the owner's office. Both Linda and Margaret were amazed by the apparent affluence of the room, although the existence of the blood on the floor together with the dentist's drill caused an immediate aversion to the eyes. As promised, Stan and Linda were drawn to the magnificent desk, which from its size had to offer a hiding place of interest. Margaret's gaze, true to form was drawn to the oak panelling of one of the walls.

Mark had an overall curiosity about the size of the

room. It did not take Linda long to discover that in order to have a thorough search of the desk, she was able to get the whole of her body into the side unoccupied by drawers. Although she found several internal keyed cabinets, nothing of interest was found. Stan was luckier in finding a few drawers of a secretive nature but they too, looked as though they had been emptied immediately prior to a hurried escape from the room. He was, however, interested in a small strip of paper which had been left, carelessly, under-neath one of the drawers. A telephone number, apparently written in a hurry, contained a prefix number identifying Inverness.

"I'll get someone in Inverness to give me the address." said Mark. "I've got a good pal at the Station and he should be able to give me the address surreptitiously and quickly if it's a listed number."

"But if it's a listed number wouldn't it be a better idea if we immediately checked all the numbers in the Inverness telephone book." quipped Linda with a wide grin on her face.

"I agree." replied Stan. "If we do it that way we can perhaps glean something very quickly and the winner need not buy a drink on the following day."

"Much as I would like to join in the fun, quickly come and see this," said Margaret excitedly. "If I prise open two separate sections of this beading here, I get a movement of a whole section of the panelling. If the panelling above is given similar treatment there has to be, from the shape alone, a doorway in this part of the wall."

Stan and Mark dashed across the room. Mark had quickly extracted his gun from his pocket. The two of them, under the guidance of Margaret, slowly pulled the panelling forward. As Margaret had suspected it was attached to a flat door panel which was now opening onto a passage, indicating a darkened cavity. Mark, gripping his gun and lit by Stan, holding his torch, led the way. The two girls followed.

"I've just had a thought." said Stan. "We've never had a real confirmation that the owner of the house has been captured. No one, except me, has actually seen him. Of the prisoners, he's never been specifically shown to any of us. It's possible that we are heading for a new hiding place or, alternatively, that he has already escaped. Anyway let's keep moving. It's pretty cold down here. With a cold draught like this I shouldn't be surprised to find that this simply leads outside. A likely route that our affluent owner has taken and that he is now being driven into Inverness. I say, Mark, I've got the feeling that this track is slowly descending further into the ground. Can you see anything when I twirl the torch?"

"No, not really. There is a slight decline to be seen but this probably has something to do with the original building. We are, undoubtedly, below ground level and I expect that further along we shall start ascending. Hey! Wait! Hold on, I'm slipping forward. It's muddy."

"Quick, here's my hand. Grab it." shrieked Stan. But he was too late, they all started down a slippery slope that would lead to God alone knew where.

The sequel to everything that had happened was beginning. Covered with mud, Mark had the sensation of being dragged down into the den of some prehistoric monster. The thought that this was some awful nightmare flashed through his mind.

"No! No!" He cried in shock. The squirming form of Stan tumbled down upon him, and behind them but close together came the two screaming women. If any of them survived, it had to be that this ordeal would be in their mind on their death bed.

Stan's torch was no longer a lantern to show them the way. Mark's sense of fun was of no avail. They were in Hell! Margaret, in desperation, was reciting the Lord's Prayer.

After what seemed an eternity, the foursome slithered to a halt, their bodies merged together like some kind of multi-limbed creature from Swamp Island. Amazingly, none of them was badly hurt, despite the ordeal. They all stood up and tried to brush themselves off and start all over again.

Linda, desperately searching in the pocket of her jacket, came upon the small torch that she had brought. There was something under one of her feet, that was, if nothing else, irritating. She shone the light on it and then let out an ear-piercing scream. She was standing on the skull of some long gone, long dead person. Margaret, seeing the terror that was tormenting her, wrapped her arms around her shoulders and held her tightly.

Meanwhile, Stan and Mark tried to sort out the place in which they appeared to be trapped. Stan found his torch, which gave them the chance to examine the place in which they were now confined. It was more of a cave than a cell and, if that were so, it might have belonged to a tribe of Stone Age forbears, likely to have been discovered when the original house was built. Shaped in the form of a circle there was an inadequate number of visible stones to support a theory that, at one time, it was actually occupied. To discover more, it was obvious that spades, hammers and a range of modern equipment were needed. Stan and Mark also, soon realised, that it was truly impossible, without scaling equipment to climb up to the point of entrance.

Suddenly a voice beamed out from some form of transmitter. It had an air of sardonic pleasure designed to humiliate its listener. Without hesitation Stan said.

"That's the swine who owns this building."

"How nice, dear Stan, to have the opportunity to speak to you once more. You have your dear friends with you, too. All of you are here to die, but it is a well appointed punishment. You have brought to death many of my followers, too. It is a most appropriate farewell. Quite enjoyable, I think. Sayad, my employee for so many years, has died. Killed by you, Stan. But he will be pleased too. Perhaps it will not be an agreeable welcome when he greets your arrival. I am leaving you now to satisfy my pleasure at training warriors from the ancient land of Sinai."

"What a stupid idiot he is. We can get out of here." said Stan.

"Yes and we'll do it right away." said Margaret. "I have my mobile phone with me."

"I've got mine with me too!" remarked Mark, laughing.

"If you don't mind I'll use mine first, Mark."

"Hello David. This is Margaret. Sorry to trouble you but the guy who owns the house which we have searched has imprisoned us in a cave actually below the building.

We need help immediately. Access to the passageway is by a door in the panelling of his room in the cellars. Because of its antiquity we can't get out. Linda, Stan and Mark are with me. Best wishes."

"Hello Dave, Mark speaking. I hope you are keeping well. It's some time since we had a chat but I need your help very quickly. I'm imprisoned, with others, in the cell of a house way up in the hills north of Gairloch. Our rescue is, hopefully, under way. I need to find, urgently, the address of a property in Inverness with this telephone number. If you are unable to contact me quickly and the occupants appear to be associated with, or belong to, the terrorists of the north, can you detain them. One of them could be my gaoler!"

"Hi! Mark, I hope you get away quickly. I'll start the telephone search right away and let you know. I have your mobile number. Have a good escape. I'll have a dram ready!"

"Are you feeling any better, Linda dear? Here, rest your head on my shoulders, we'll not be here for long now that we have others working for us."

"Oh, Stan, and all of you, I'm so sorry for acting like a child. It was the shock of falling I think. Mind you, I'm not sure that I will go looking for hidden cupboards and secret rooms again."

"Of course you will," said Margaret, "that's the fun of it. Horrid though this is, there's an air of intrigue about it. Our friend on his transmitter was pretty prompt in speaking to us. How did he know about our fall within minutes of its happening? Apart from Stan we might not be able to recognise his voice. You, Stan, have had the advantage of watching him have his coffee. That's a great privilege. In his mind, at that stage of course, he had the thought that you would not be leaving the dentist!"

"Oh! Margaret. Please shut up! I'm doing my best to wipe out that event from the centre of my thoughts. If you ladies were not here my talk would be crowned by the highest peak of obscenity imaginable!"

"That alone would be a damned sight better than some of the words you use all the time!" said Mark. "Oh that's my mobile. Hi! Dave, any luck? You have? Ah, that's great. What? Donald Smith? He's also known as Abdullah Mohammed. Just one minute. I'll have a quick word with Stan."

"'Yes, Mark. We've got to get him pretty quickly. Tell him right away if he can do it. Grab anyone else too, please."

"Yes Dave, grab them all, right away if you can. We'll be along as soon as we get away. As a matter of etiquette it would be as well to let Dave Watson know as soon as you can. All the best."

Stan smiled, almost secretly to Margaret. He never said anything but her general knowledge and investigative interests pointed to something more than hospital care for others.

Suddenly lumps of earth began to fall on them. They all looked at each other in supreme horror. Was this a natural occurrence or was it all planned for their destruction? Then they heard voices.

"Are you all right down there? We've got a rope ladder on the way down. It shouldn't take too long and then we'll be with you. If you can keep your hands over your eyes, it might help. The ladder keeps swinging, causing some of the soil to drop."

"Listen!" Urged Stan. "That's the voice of Dave!" The foursome began to cheer like mad.

"Soon, you'll all be allowed to have a sumptuous bath, not together of course, but one containing an excess of soapy water. Better still a shower, the water of which has a velocity of immense speed."

"You mean running water!" muttered Mark.

"Quick!" shouted Margaret, "see the bottom of the hanging ladder. You can just see it in the beam of my torch."

"That's great, Margaret. Who's going first?"

"I'll go first to make sure that there's nothing at the lop liable to make anyone slip. Ah! Here it is. Good luck to the rest of you."

"You'll be safe, Mark. I'll keep the bottom from swinging." It did not take long before the girls were climbing to the welcoming hands above and Stan waved goodbye to the horror below.

Dave gave the women, a much needed hug of joy causing tears to run down their cheeks. Turning to Mark he thanked him for the quick information on the possibility of some of the terrorists in Inverness being caught. As yet, he'd received no information but it should not be long before they heard something. He quickly called for Linda and Margaret to be given bathrooms where hot baths and drinks were awaiting them.

For the men, large glasses of whisky were already there before direction was given to them as to the whereabouts of the showers.

It was some time before news was heard of the occupants of the address in Inverness. There were two men and a woman. No interrogation of them had yet been pursued. They would await the arrival of David and Stan Watson and others who might have information. David said that he would allow Mark, Linda and Margaret to come along in recognition of their experiences. The helicopter was still available and he arranged for their immediate transport to Inverness.

A police car was awaiting them at Inverness Airport. They arrived at the suspected house in record time and were shown into the large room where the suspects were being held. As it happened, they were not tethered in any way to their seats.

Stan's entry to the room enabled him to have a good sight of the owner of the house from whence they came. He was a person of great physical strength but added to this was a glare depicting an immense possession of arrogance. Stan felt immediately that the look of hatred was reserved entirely for him.

A uniformed Policeman guarded him on one side of the room.

David looked at him with a feeling of great joy when he entered the room. Here was a man who thought that it was his right to bully others and now there had to be an end to what he thought was a given right to possess others. Now, he looked at David with a face exhibiting a great hatred. It was clear that he wanted to destroy David as well as his cousin, Stan. On his part, David noticed that he wore no cufflinks, which might have held him back should he attempt to escape.

Then it all happened so quickly. What appeared to be a simple putting aside of his hair turned out to be a powerful sweep of his fist into the face of the Policeman. This was only the beginning because it was accompanied by a heavy blow into the side of Stan's face and for David a ferocious kick into one of his shins. Then, to the amazement of his audience, this was followed by a quick grip of the door handle and he was through the door, believed by all, to be holding him in the room.

The immediate thought of the occupants of the room was that he could be captured before he escaped but that was no avail. Although there was a staunch search in the city of Inverness and in isolated parts he was not found. Complete security was now achieved for the two prisoners remaining.

An instant examination was given to Stan's face by Margaret. She thought that his nose was likely to be broken and called for assistance from the hospital in Inverness. Despite his injury, Stan was able, without any hesitation, to say. "The man who has just attacked me is the owner of the Highland House. He spoke to me before arrangements were put in force to kill me."

With great joy he pointed to the other man. "That is the guy whom I met at Tallinn. He is the man responsible for so much terrorism. I shall make myself available to give evidence when it is needed."

Linda accompanied Stan to the hospital where immediate attention was given, but fortunately his nose was not broken.

They left to go to the hotel where arrangements had

been made for their accommodation. Soon after their arrival. Mark and Margaret arrived to confirm that they would be staying there too. Mark insisted that they went down to the bar where drinks would be made available immediately. He also said that on the morrow David would be joining them too.

It turned out that their expected visit to the bar was not as great as they had previously thought. Mark had now begun to call their missing man 'bully boy' but none of them was able to achieve a party of great joy or to make sensible suggestions as to where an arrest could be made. Fatigue had unfortunately taken over and a suggestion to part was immediately adopted.

CHAPTER TWENTY FIVE

Over the ensuing days, Stan and David held press conferences the length and breadth of the country to try and glean information as to the whereabouts of the mysterious 'Smith' and the even more mysterious X. But they had concealed their identities so well that no pertinent information was forthcoming. And even the interrogation of the terrorists who were captured did not help: they could not or would not shed a light on the subject: the loyalty – brought on by a common goal or more likely an intense fear – had made them keep whatever they knew to themselves.

The disappointment was enormous for all concerned. But perhaps in the weeks to come, especially after their upcoming appearance on Crimewatch UK, some pertinent information as to the fugitives' whereabouts would come to light.

Stan was like the rest of the people involved in the tragedies – completely mystified by the disappearance of the obvious leaders and instigators of the plot – especially the man they knew only by the moniker of X! The only sighting of X, who owned the big house in the Highlands (bought, no doubt, from ill-gotten terrorist gains), described him as being from 'a middle eastern country'. There was not an inkling of his name, his whereabouts, or where he really originated from – and the last verifiable sighting of him was in Inverness, probably on the way to the airport and thence to the safety of the shelter of his cohorts.

Stan knew already that the whole of the country had been on Red Alert, with airports, seaports, and private airfields all under intense scrutiny, and anyone with any information would come forward to give an identity, but still nothing. Even Inverness itself, which was an obvious place for information and a possible identification, revealed nothing. The country's police forces had issued descriptions, artists' impressions were circulated on all the TV networks, and even Allied countries were on the alert. But STILL they could not be found.

What was certain was that they had not 'retired' – terrorists never do, they just continue to kill until they themselves are killed. At this very moment they are probably in the process of setting up a new, more motivated, more virulent, and more deadly terrorist cell in another part of the country. Perhaps preparing to strike at any moment of any day of any week at any location in the country – perhaps somewhere near you. Then they will deal out death and destruction to innocent men, women and children alike. Indiscriminate massacre – and the more deaths they cause, the merrier they will be.

CHAPTER TWENTY SIX

Linda and Stan were alone in their hotel bedroom. Linda had been quiet for a while and then she said. "Stan, there's something I want to tell you!"

"No you can't. I'm speaking first. Will you marry me, please?"

"Yes, of course I will. I've been hoping that you are ready to ask me now that our troubles seem to be over. Oh! Just wait a moment. I know that you have plenty of money. I haven't. Let me know how much you will be giving me!"

"Of course, but it will depend on how much you eat and how many times you clean the house!"

"I'll keep a record!"

Stan took her in his arms and gave her a loving kiss. He then said "I love you so much but what do you want to tell me?"

"Oh! Stan, I'm going to have a baby!"

"Linda dear, it's what I wanted but I didn't know. Oh, this is absolutely super, darling."

There was a knock on the door. Margaret, David and Mark entered the room.

"Come on downstairs," said Dave, "we've got drinks ordered, and the waiter is hovering with the lunch menu."

"Just a minute, I've got something to tell you - no, TWO things! We're going to get married *and* Linda is going to have a baby!"

With that, a cheer broke out and Margaret said. "I've never said anything, Linda. I've really wanted to congratulate you for some time but lying at the bottom of a cave seemed neither the right time nor the right place!"

"'Twas then that I thought you knew!" laughed Linda. "God bless you all."

"OK" said Stan. "We'll have a big party and you are all invited. We like presents too! You can bring your children too!"

BrightSpark Publishing
.co.uk

Bookshop and Publisher

Unit 11, The Wards, Elgin, IV30 6AA

(Behind Po'Teak in Scorpion Computers' former unit)

Elgin (01343) 544336; Mobile 07967 178224

The Wee Shop With BIG Bargains

£5

A fast paced mystery/crime/courthouse drama, it examines criminal justice, disability rights and mental illness.

£5

Illegal drugs, murder, good guys, bad guys, thrills, spills, laughs, and a new lovable anti-hero who is determined to right all wrongs, combine in a yarn in the style of Leslie 'The Saint' Charteris!

£5

Vampires and their hunters are waging a bloody war in the streets we ourselves may stray down!

The Thoughtful Throttler

A comic combination of Fantasy, Philosophy, Murder, and Horror! Unmissable!

£5

Sci-Fi and Fantasy merge to form a yarn of past, present and what may yet be. Intriguing, thought-provoking, and engrossing.

£5

A thrilling Sci-Fi epic with betrayal, danger and environmental concerns!.

£5

TONY BARON

R.I.P. HUMANITY

A spellbinding, brutal and unnerving horror novel dealing with the last few survivors in a world torn apart by disease. A 'Day of The living dead' for the 21st Century!

£5

£5   £5

Submissions very welcome:
For more details, phone, 01343 544336,
pop into the shop,
or visit www.BrightSparkPublishing.co.uk

**All our own books are
published and printed
entirely in-house.
Most available in-store;
all can be ordered online.**

A wonderful mystical tale merging fantasy, horror and 'coming-of-age' in one truly spellbinding yarn.

£5

An entertaining eclectic collection of fantasy, sci-fi and horror short yarns.

The quest: Find sections of a matter transmitter that are scattered over a continent. Fail, and the only human colony-planet dies

£5

Our Current and Forthcoming Imprints:

BRIGHTSPARK ÉCOSSE

BrightSpark Crime

BRIGHTSPARK HORROR

BRIGHTSPARK SCI-FI

BrightSpark Fantasy

BrightSpark Biographies

BRIGHTSPARK CULT TV AND FILM

BrightSpark Noir

BRIGHTSPARK BAIRNS

BRIGHTSPARK CLASSICS

- -

You can order any of our books from our website - www.brightsparkpublishing.co.uk - or in our shop (where you can also get big name books at 50% of their RRP!), but if you prefer you can post us this form, together with a cheque for the appropriate amount made payable to BrightSpark Publishing, and we'll send them out to - P+P free.

TITLE	QUANTITY	PRICE	TOTAL
		GRAND TOTAL	

NAME	
ADDRESS	